Fran, The Second Time Around

Amy L. Bernstein

Second printing by IngramSpark/Lightning Source.

Acknowledgments

Das, Lama Surya, *Letting Go of the Person You Used to Be: Lessons on Change, Loss, and Spiritual Transformation.* New York: Broadway Books, 2003. [First trade paperback ed., Nov. 2004]

Follmi, Danielle and Olivier, *Offerings: Buddhist Wisdom for Every Day.* New York: Stewart, Tabor & Chang [undated, unpaginated]

Gibson, William, *The Miracle Worker.* New York: Pocket Books, 2002.

Martin,Philip, *The Zen Path Through Depression.* San Francisco: Harper Collins, 1999. [first paperback ed., 2000]

Shoshanna, Brenda, *Zen Miracle: Finding Peace in an Insane World.* New York: John Wiley & Sons, 2003.

Part I

Fall 2007

Chapter 1

The alarm is about to go off. I know it is, because I set it myself last night. I watch the little colon blink—the vertical dots that separate the hour from the minutes. 6:42 AM. Blink, blink, blink. Staring at the clock, I open and shut my eyes to see if I can blink in sync, so that when my eyes are open, for a split second, the colon looks solid—like it isn't blinking at all. When my eyes are shut, the colon blinks off. I find I can do this about three times in a row before the sequence gets messed up. Is this like meditating? Maybe. Sort of. Peter would probably say no. Yeah, I'm sure he would.

At six forty-five, I'll hear the whoosh of ocean waves. That's my alarm. No loud buzzer for me. No radio, either. What if I were to wake up to a song I really hated? That could get the whole day off to a bad start. Ruin my karma, or something. Anyway, since I'm already awake, I reach over and slap off the alarm. No ocean lapping the shore this morning. No noise of any kind, really, except a loud rushing in my ears.

I'm not nervous, no, not nervous at all. I can do this. Anyone can do this. Millions of people my age, and older, and younger, will do this, today.

As I once did, without a second thought.

I sit up and swing my legs over the side of the bed. The pads of my feet stick slightly to the wooden floor. It's another humid September day, the first Tuesday after Labor Day. I glance around my bedroom for no particular reason, except maybe to stall. My big meditation pillow, soft and brown, with an indentation where my butt rests—think of a dog bed, and you'll get the idea— sits on the floor in the corner, next to my closet. If the pillow could speak, it would tell me, 'Come on over, sit, rest, clear your mind before the day starts.' But I don't want to do that now. Maybe

1

later. Maybe tonight. I'm good at that—putting things off—a champion procrastinator. You know the saying, *Never put off 'til tomorrow what you can do today.* I'm the opposite. If something can wait, let it. If there's stuff you don't want to do, or don't want to think about, put it somewhere else. In some corner of your brain, stashed away like those stupid old tennis trophies you won at summer camp—the cheesy plastic painted to look like gold. They're stuffed on a back shelf in an old closet in our guest room, along with all the other stuff you can't believe you once cared about—a Girl Scout Brownie sash filled with glued-on badges, class photos from elementary school, all the kids smiling for the camera with their goofy, gap-toothed grins.

As for the other stuff—the stuff that's in your head that you'd just as soon throw out—it's in a closet too, and you try to keep it locked up, only sometimes, when you can't help it, the closet door creaks open and stuff leaks out. But you don't want to look at it, so you stuff it all back in as fast as you can. I'm a champion at that, too.

Watch the colon on the clock: on, off, on, off. Now blink...blink now! Now! That's it. Hold onto the illusion for as long as you can....

OK, that's enough of that. Up. Wash. Brush. Dress. Just do it. This is an episode of *Survivor.* You're one of the strongest, most resourceful contestants left on the island. Nothing but tough muscle and an even tougher attitude. A skin as thick as, I don't know, an elephant's hide. Ready to handle anything. The million dollar prize will be yours if only.... No, it's *Fear Factor.* You're not afraid of heights. Not afraid to eat worms, or to be buried alive. . . . Cue the sound. Cue the lights. We need some atmosphere here, people! Land of the living, and all. And the silence—it's enough already. The head-rushing white noise has ended, anyway. So tunes are needed. I reach over to the Mac on my desk and click on iTunes.

...Summer has come and passed
The innocent can never last
Wake me up when September ends...

A fresh start. A clean slate. That's what Mom said as I headed out the door to catch the annoyingly bright and infantile school bus. *No one knows you, or anything about you*, she said. *You can be who you are—whoever you want to be.* Now isn't that just great. I have the privilege of beginning ninth grade, the start of my high school career—or lack of career, more likely—as a complete zero, a nobody. No history, no personality, no best friend. Tracy is out of the picture after, let's see, eleven years of tried-and-true, best-buds-til-we-die-friendship. Yeah, well things change in ways you can't imagine.

So nobody to sit with at lunch, nobody to hang with at lockers, or pass a note to in chem class. No chance of landing the lead in the class play 'cause they didn't see me play Helen Keller two years ago, did they? No, they did not. And my IM list? Pathetic. This will shock you: the list is three names long. And they're all first cousins. No, I'm not a total antisocial loser. I've just, let's say, lost touch with some people recently.

Including Peter. Big round, soft, Peter. The Sta-Puff Marshmallow Man. But that's by choice. In my face every day for almost a year. Now, nowhere, or who knows where? It's strange: He knew a version of me: Fran 1.0. Am I still that version? The one with all the bugs in it? Or was I secretly upgraded during the night by a band of stealthy science geeks. *We'll make her better, faster, stronger....the new, improved ninth grade model.* Anyway, the chapter on Peter is closed. He's like a pair of crutches that you need while your leg is in a cast—but once the leg is healed, well, the crutches get tossed away. Or thrown into the closet. Let Peter handle Peter now, wherever he is. Peter the Wise. Peter the Good. Peter the Patient. He doesn't have to handle me anymore.

So long, Buddha. It's been nice to know ya.

3

What Mom didn't say, I notice, is that I can be who I was. Past tense. No, I cannot climb into a time machine, turn the clock back, and be who I was. I can't climb out of my head, which is now filled with stuff I don't want in there. Stuff I want to put into that closet and then throw away the key. Peter would say, *Forget about it and let go. Be in the moment. Live in the moment. The past is the river that's already flowing into the ocean, way long gone. There is only now.*

The moment, now, is a bus that pulls up alongside an enormous red brick building with a flat tar-black roof. Westmore High School. More what? A generic name for a generic-looking building. It looks anonymous—and so do I. I clomp off the bus with everyone else and walk through the bright green double-doors. Nobody seems to be paying any attention to me, which figures, since I don't know a soul.

"Excuse me, you look lost," says a voice to my left. "Do you know where your House is?" The voice belongs to a woman about Mom's age, a few inches shorter than I. She's got a clipboard and that open-eyed, helpful look adults get sometimes, when they want to steer you somewhere. "House" is what they call a homeroom at this school. I think it's kind of juvenile, personally, for ninth graders to have to report to a "house," but them's the rules. I didn't make 'em, I'm not gonna break 'em. Not yet, anyway. *A fresh start.*

"I've got Christa Neal. Room 39, it says." I glance down at a piece of paper I've been clutching since I got onto the bus. Not nervous, no, just making sure. My purple backpack slips half-way off my left shoulder. It's too light, this first day of school; no textbooks or notebooks yet. Just a Hewlett-Packard calculator and a brown bag with a tuna fish sandwich and I don't remember what else. I don't like cafeteria food—it's mushy and tasteless. So I packed my own lunch, just to be safe.

"Go through those double doors at the end of the corridor, turn left, then left again, and you'll find 39," the born-to-be-helpful lady tells me. I don't really think I should need directions, at this point in my life, but after all, I was only here once before, when I was checking the place out with Mom and Dad. *All part of the healing process. Part of moving on,* they said. *You've got to get back on track, Fran.* . . . *'It's all about what's happening right now, Fran.'* Peter again. *'Not yesterday, not last year. Only now.* . . . '

I find Room 39 without any trouble and take a seat at the back, naturally. Where else is a new girl going to sit? Oh, sure, there may be girls who would plop down right in front, then turn around and smile and look around at everyone, and try to catch somebody's attention—anybody's—to prove they exist, that they're conversation-worthy. Scouting out the cutest guy, the one who's built like a jock but also looks really smart, like he can do it all. This sort of girl would probably be blonde, wearing blue eye shadow and a miniskirt and those cute little low-heeled pumps you see everywhere. But that girl wouldn't be me. I've got light brown hair knotted into a French braid down my back, a black tee shirt and low-cut jeans with a big tear at the right ankle, and Paul Frank flip-flops. OK, I put on a dab of dark lipstick this morning, sort of maroony, but that's it. I might look the part—but I'm not feeling it, as my old drama teacher would say. Sometimes, I realize now, she sounded a lot like Peter—but I didn't know Peter then.

"I'm not feeling it from you, Fran," she'd tell me, a disembodied voice lodged somewhere in the first or second row of the auditorium, behind the glare of the stage light. *"Experience the emotion now, right now, in the present. Make it real,"* she'd say, waving her arms, as if that could help. *"Helen is angry, frustrated—angrier and more frustrated than she's been in her entire life. You've felt that way, surely? Find it, and use it. Are you with me, Fran?"* Yes, I'd tell her, so desperate to get this right, to show that she was right to put her trust in me. She couldn't be wrong, could she? I didn't beat out twenty-six other girls for this chance, just to blow it, did I? I was only twelve—soon to turn thirteen, but God help me, I desperately wanted to be Helen Keller—well, at least to *feel* Helen Kellerish. Or at any rate, to

5

convince *her* that I did. But what could he expect from an innocent twelve-year-old, who knew nothing, absolutely nothing, about the ways of the world, let alone a deaf, dumb, and blind girl born more than a century ago?

I'm snapped back to the present by a high-pitched voice.

"Good morning. I'm Christa Neal," says the woman at the front of the room. She's wearing a weird sort of plaid skirt and has short, curly red hair that clashes with the red in the skirt. The room settles down in slow motion, as backpacks drop to the floor and people sink to their seats. "I'm going to be handing out locker assignments, where you can store your backpacks and such. After today, you'll report here every day at mid-morning, after second period, and I'll go over announcements and anything else you need to know. If you have any questions or concerns about your classes or your teachers, I'm here to help. That's the whole point of House. All you have to do is ask. Oh, and one more thing." Christa Neal then takes roll and hands out nametags, which we're asked to wear for the first two weeks of school during House, until she learns our names.

This is sooo lame. We all know it. I roll my eyes and catch my neighbor doing the same thing—and for a split second, I feel like I might actually belong here with this bunch of strangers. The girl whose glance I catch is sitting next to me. She's thin with short, razor-straight black hair that swings above her shoulders. She's got the shiniest hair I've ever seen, and she's wearing a Bruce Springsteen tee shirt. I don't really know Springsteen's music, or even what I think of it, but I find I'm willing to give her the benefit of the doubt. Suddenly, she frowns, her dark eyebrows forming a ridge.

"Hey, are you new? You must be new. I don't think I've ever seen you before."

"Yeah, that's right. I just transferred. Kind of weird, huh, starting over in high school?" I reply.

"I guess," she shrugs. "Well I'm Cynthia. Not Cyn, not Cindy. Cynthia Li. That's L-I. Not L-E-E. OK? God, that bugs me, when people give you a nickname without even asking. Anyway. . . ."

"Fran," I reply. "Not Francine or Frances. Just Fran. Singer. Like, um, Beyoncé. And I agree." And then I smile, I actually smile. I had almost forgotten how easy it could be. Suddenly, I'm blushing, and I hope Cynthia doesn't notice. I'm not blushing because of her, but because of what my dad had said to me a few hours earlier, before I left for school. I was dawdling in my room, of course, trying to find a reason not to come down and face the day. I was so desperate I even made my bed, which I never do, pulling up the sheet and the quilt nice and tight, folding them back smoothly, and lining my pillows up just so—including my rainbow-colored "peace" pillow that I bought at a state fair when I was nine; it's got a giant peace sign in the middle. Making the bed—at least that was something in my control. . . .

"Fran! Come down! You don't want to be late for your first day!" Dad shouted from the bottom of the stairs. What right did he have to be such an eager beaver? He wasn't the one who had to face down an entire school. Who wouldn't want to be late? Or not late, exactly, but in suspended animation. Maybe I could just stare at my blinking clock all day. Not really here, not really there. Sort of between the worlds of *must* and *should*. But Dad wouldn't really get that. He's the sort of person who's all about getting things done. The very opposite of a procrastinator like me. He'll mow our front lawn the second the grass is about an inch high. He's a building contractor. I've never really been sure what that means, exactly, but I think what it boils down to is that he makes sure that new office buildings and shopping malls and such get built on time, and that they don't cost more than they're supposed to. He always likes to say he "makes the trains run on time," but I've never really understood that, since I'm pretty sure his work doesn't have anything to do with trains. Anyway, he says his work is like a game of chess: he's always trying to stay several moves ahead of everybody else, so that if anything looks like it could go wrong, he

7

can fix it before it does. I don't really get how you can fix a problem before it happens, but that's what he says.

Anyway, I dabbed on the lipstick at the last minute so that I looked sort of finished, and went down. And there they were: Dad, Mom, and Toby, my 11 year-old brother. A real study in nonchalance: looking like they didn't have a care in the world. Like this was like any other day. Toby, in sixth grade, was in the same elementary school he'd always attended. No switcheroo for him. Now that he is at the top of the school, this first day was a triumph for him. He was king of the roost—or at least, a member of the dominating class. The sixth graders loved lording it over the little ones. I remembered that. How I wish . . . never mind. Don't go there.

Mom was standing at the counter in a sort of trance, slowly mixing blueberry yogurt into a small bowl of the cereal she liked— some disgusting combination of twigs and oat flakes, or something. Dad was standing by the sink, drinking coffee and checking messages on his Blackberry. Toby was reading an *X-Men* comic book and shoving Frosted Flakes into his mouth so fast, the milk dribbled out, down his chin.

"Eat, Fran, before you go," Mom said, breaking out of her trance and turning to me. Typical. Did somebody pass a law that breakfast was a requirement? Could you send a kid to jail for refusing to eat breakfast?

"Mmm, not hungry," I replied. "I'm fixing lunch, though," I said, getting busy with a can of tuna. Mom and Dad exchanged a brief glance. They thought I didn't catch it, but I did.

"Take a granola bar, at least. Maybe you'll eat it later," Mom said, pulling an oatmeal raisin granola bar out of a big box— she bought them in bulk—stored in a sliding drawer next to the stove. I took it and shoved it into my backpack; it was far easier than refusing.

"What's your first class this morning, hon?" Dad asked. He had put away his Blackberry, and was finishing his coffee.

"Uh, math, I think."

"Does this school have a varsity basketball team?" Toby asked, his spoon clinking in the empty bowl.

"Put that in the sink, Toby, and rinse it," Mom said. "I'm not doing it for you." Toby shoved the bowl down the table—in the general direction of the sink.

"How should I know?" I said. "And why would I care?"

"You probably don't, but I thought I might go to a game, or something, this fall," Toby said in a slightly raspy, husky voice. He often sounded like he had a frog in his throat, or maybe his nose was stopped up. "Maybe cheer the team. I gotta find out what they're called, though. The Westmore Wonks? The Westmore Wimps? The Wispy-Crispies?" Toby let out a big "Hah!," which was his way of laughing at his own sorry jokes. I ignored this childish outburst, as always. When Toby was little, like three or so, whenever he cried over something—like maybe his favorite Thomas the Tank engine thingy had broken—he'd come running to me and put his arms around my waist (that was about as high as he could reach) and bury his wet little face in my stomach. I would usually lean down and soothe him, in my best Mommy voice. But those days are long over. I can't really figure out what he's all about now. For that matter, I can't seem to figure anybody out anymore, least of all me.

"I've got to scoot," Dad said, looking at his watch. "They're beginning to put the skin on the Fowler Building today, and I've got to get to Wilmington A.S.A.P." He put his coffee cup in the sink, picked up his beat-up leather briefcase, and gave Mom a quick peck on the cheek. I tried to picture what skin looked like, stretched out on a building.

"Everybody OK here?" he asked in a casual tone, his eyes skipping around to each of us—me in particular, of course.

"Will you make it back for dinner?" Mom asked. "I thought you said you would."

"If the beltway traffic isn't too bad, I should be back around six-thirty. Want me to pick anything up?"

"No," Mom said. "I'm only showing one house today. That little one over on Keswick. So I'll have time." Mom sells houses—sort of. I mean, she does it part-time and it seems like hardly anyone ever buys the houses she shows them. I don't know why, exactly. Maybe she picks bad houses, or something. Maybe the houses smell, or the kitchen's too small, or whatever.

"What's A-S-A-P?" Toby asked.

"What, Toby? Please put your bowl in the sink, like I asked."

"Dad said he had to be somewhere A-S-A-P. What's that?"

"As soon as possible"—Mom, Dad, and I said in unison, which made us all burst out laughing, including Toby. Suddenly, the kitchen went still. The silence lasted only for a second or two—but long enough so that we all noticed. You could hear the coffee pot gurgling. It had been a long time since we had laughed together as a family. Too long. Mom, Dad, and Toby all looked at me, as if on secret command. I turned around quickly and put my tuna sandwich into a paper bag. Dad came around and put his hands on my shoulders and gave them a squeeze.

"Good luck today," he said softly. "Everything's going to be OK, pumpkin." That's the moment I remembered when I met Cynthia. He said everything was going to be OK. And maybe it would. But I hadn't really felt able to count on anything being the way it was supposed to be—or turning out the way I expected it to—in a really, really long time, so I wasn't going to get my hopes up too high. I was definitely going to take a wait-and-see attitude.

As the Buddha said—according to Peter, anyway—everything put together falls apart.

Chapter 2

Whooosh. Whooosh. That pesky alarm again. The ocean waves rolling up against the shore. The school year is barely six weeks old, and the ocean has awakened me every one of those school days. It's supposed to be soothing, but it's turning out to be annoying. The first thing I do as sleep leaks away: Feel for the old dread weighing down my chest, like a warm cat that's been sleeping on me. Only not half as cozy. And it's there, oh, it's always there. Did anyone honestly thing a change of scenery—a new school, a new group of potential friends—was going to make it all magically disappear? I lie there, scanning my room in the dim early dawn, as if looking for some good news. And I find it—a tidbit, anyway. I didn't have the usual dream, the Really Bad One, where the same thing happens over and over again and I can't change a thing. Anyway, I didn't have that dream. Instead, I dreamed that Cynthia and I were in the Towson mall, wandering in and out of Delia's and American Eagle, and some other stores. We sit on a bench, and I'm feeling—this is in the dream, of course—like there's no place else I want to be, besides right here in the good old mall with my new best friend. The girl with the perfect almond-shaped eyes and shiny black hair that sort of swings from side to side. I like that. So different from my heavy, coarse, brown hair that I can't really do anything with except put into a long braid to keep it out of the way—like a horse's tail banging away at flies. I guess it's silly to admire somebody because of their hair. Cynthia was just born with it. Luck of the draw. It doesn't make her a good person, or anything. But still. We're sitting there on one of those pathetic benches in the corridor, where tired old men usually sit waiting for their wives to finish shopping. And she turns to me and says, "I know all about it. It's OK. Don't worry about it anymore. You can't change the past. You're somebody else now." She says this, and I just turn to her with what I imagine is this astonished look on my face. What does she know? Who told her? Who—or what—does she think I am?

I'm remember this dream—and for a split second, I can't remember what day it is—no, what year it is. My ceiling fan is whirring slowly. The last days of Indian summer have kept even the evenings warm, as Halloween approaches. My heart is pounding, and I'm sweating through my tee shirt nightie.

I'm not going back, I'm going forward. I'm not going back, I'm going forward. I'm not going back, I'm going forward.

These words race through my head, over and over. Like a chant—but nothing the Buddha or the Dalai Lama would recommend, I'm pretty sure. You know how, when you're watching a DVD, you can race through any bits you don't want to see, or jump backwards through scenes, through time, until you get to some part you want to see again? I wish you could do that in real life—just fast-forward when you needed to. Or skip backwards, maybe even erase whole scenes, as if they'd never happened. But damn, you just can't. Real life isn't that convenient. You're forced to take it one slow day at a time. Whether you want to or not.

I get out of bed and settle down onto my velvety brown meditation pillow. Seems as good a time as any, and I haven't done this in ages, anyway. Peter said I should try to meditate part of every day. But come on, get real. I have to be in the mood. The dream was so vivid, but it kind of slowed me down, which is a good thing. So here I sit. Legs crossed. Eyes closed.

Sitting quietly, bring your attention to your breath.

Feel the rise and fall of your belly as you breathe in and out. Follow the inhalations and exhalations for a few minutes.

Now begin to focus on your breath as you breathe out.

Feel the air going out and dissolving into the space around you.

12

"Fran! Come on, we're gonna miss the bus!" Toby has burst into my room like a dirty tornado, leaving a trail of I don't know what—Pop Tart crumbs, or something. Meditation is over for today. For all the good it did me. I get dressed, grab a granola bar to keep Mom happy, and lug my backpack and myself to school.

Almost everything inside Westmore this time of year is brown and orange. Somebody has strung paper leaves that are supposed to remind you of autumn, up and down the hallway near my locker. I don't really get the point. If you walk outside, you can see the real thing—maple trees turning orange and yellow, and brown, dry leaves crunching underfoot. I don't notice them much, though once in a while, when the sun is really strong in the afternoon, when I step outside to catch the bus, the leaves seem to glow, to become almost transparent. I'm making an effort, I really am, to notice stuff like this: the good stuff, even if it's trivial or sentimental, or whatever. I point out this glow thing to Cynthia one day—she's the kind of person you can stay stuff like that to, and she doesn't think it's too weird. She looked up and squinted, and said it looked nice, like a postcard she'd seen of Vermont in October. What I don't tell her is that the glowing leaves also remind me of death. That the leaves glow because they are thinning, losing life force, getting weak. Preparing to die.

And no one, and no force of nature, can stop them. Death comes, again and again and again.

The bell rings for first period and lockers slam shut up and down the hallway. I'm not much of a morning person, myself, but that's OK, 'cause lots of other kids have no problem making up for my quiet yawning.

"Troke, what's up, dude?" croaks the loud bass voice of a guy in my Spanish class, Brent. "Did you finish that thing last night, man? I bagged it at twelve-thirty. Couldn't take it, anymore, man."

13

"Nah, I don't know what's up with that," Troke replies. "I was blogging til like two. Sort of forgot to finish, myself." He and Brent are both big guys with long, sort of stringy brown hair down their backs. I don't know Troke's real last name. I think it's something complicated, like Trocadero. "I'm gonna ask for an extension."

"Good luck with that," Brent replies, laughing. He punches Troke in the arm. Why do guys do that? I'd get really irritated if Cynthia started punching me every time we had a conversation.

A sea of kids and notebooks jam the hallway as the second bell rings. Lots of kids hurl Starbucks cups in to the nearest trashcan. It's OK to bring your coffee in here, but you gotta finish it before you get into class. So you often see kids chugging mochas and Frappuccinos when the second bell rings. Westmore is only three blocks from this little village, where there's a Starbucks, a little book store, a dry cleaners and some other shops. So it's easy to caf up before coming to school. I don't really know yet if I like coffee. I haven't really had to time to think about it. I haven't even really been to a Starbucks. I mean, I've driven past lots of them, with my parents. But I haven't hung out there. Yet. I'm probably gonna try it soon, and see.

At lunch, I bring my nylon lunch sack to the cafeteria and scan for Cynthia. The cafeteria is loud and chaotic, as usual. Long lines for fries; kids popping change into the Coke machine.

"Fran! Here!" I spot Cynthia sitting at a beat up table that's not our usual one. We always try to sit in the back left corner, because that's where you get the best view of who's coming in to the room. But today, a bunch of guys I don't know are parked there. So I walk between tables to the other side. Cynthia's sitting with the usual crowd—well, usual to me only since September, since I'm the newbie here. There's Katie, short with blonde curls, and really sweet. Leo—short for Leonora, which I think is one of the most beautiful and romantic girl's names I've ever heard. It's a little fussy, maybe, but that's not Leo's fault. Anyway, Leo is super-smart; that's one thing you can tell about her right away.

14

And Max—a guy Max—who I think has a crush on Katie. He seems to follow her everywhere, though Katie told me last week that they're not in any of the same classes. Max is OK, really. He's not like Brent and Troke; he doesn't go around punching all the guys he talks to. And he doesn't just grunt, like they do. He holds actual conversations, at least sometimes. I've noticed that his upper arms are really muscular. I think Katie told me he plays a lot of baseball.

"Hey," Leo says as I sit down.

"Whoa, that is such a cool barrette," says Katie, fingering the wide leopard print barrette with a turquoise rhinestone in the middle, which I shoved across the top of my French brain this morning.

"Thanks," I say.

"Whatcha got?" Cynthia asks. She's got a white Styrofoam tray with a strawberry yogurt, a mangy looking apple, and a bag of salt-and-vinegar potato chips.

"The usual," I say. Tuna. A peach that's gone a little soft. One of those granola bars we never seem to run out of at home. I'll probably be starving later, but this was all I could scrape together in four minutes in the morning. I reach across to get some of Cynthia's chips.

"So anyway," Leo says, "he went out there to be by himself because he wanted to make a political statement."

"What political statement?" Cynthia asks.

"You know, like, to show that the world is too materialistic. That you don't need to be surrounded by lots of things to have a good time, or a good life, or whatever."

"I think he just didn't get along with people," says Katie. "You always make everything so complicated, Leo."

"No offense, Leo," Cynthia says, "but I think that's sort of impossible, making a political statement, because in the old days they didn't have the media so nobody would know what he was doing, anyway. He'd just end up alone."

"What—" I begin, totally lost.

15

"Thoreau," Leo says. "Henry David. In Speck's class, we gotta write a long essay about why Thoreau went off to live in a cabin on a lake by himself." Leo gathers her mass of frizzy brown hair into a pony tail and absent-mindedly wraps an elastic around the frizzy bundle.

"Oh," I say, relieved to finally get the point of the conversation. "For Richards, we have to write an essay like we're Thoreau ourselves—like we're the one going off, and explain our reasons."

"That sounds less boring," says Katie. "This Thoreau guy, I think he was just anti-social. I mean, who in their right mind is going to go off and live in an unheated cabin where there's no cable, no grocery store, stuff like that? He was a, you know, a hermit."

"Katie," Leo says, "nobody had cable or anything. It wasn't like a punishment. Though I guess, if he were doing it today, he'd have his own Web page, or he'd podcast, probably."

"They didn't know what they were missing," I add—surprising myself a little by speaking up. "I think he's the kind of guy who'd use an old quill pen and some dusty parchment, no matter what. Even if he were alive today, he probably couldn't get a wireless connection out in the woods, anyway. Besides, I think Thoreau really liked to be alone so he could think—and he wouldn't have to explain himself to anybody. Or be judged."

"Yeah, that's good," says Cynthia. Are you going to put that in your paper?"

"And also, out there by himself, he could make a mistake, and nobody would know," I add.

"What kind of mistake?" asks Max, leaning forward on the table, crumpling his Styrofoam tray. I look around the table and see them all looking at me, waiting for me to explain myself. To come up with something clever. I'm not really sure what I meant—or where to take it. They're all looking at me and I can feel my undigested lunch start to churn.

16

"Well," I begin slowly, trying really hard to keep any shakiness out of my voice. "Suppose he lights a fire one night, and the fire gets out of control, and starts spreading to the woods."

"Oooh, I like this," Max grins. "Go on. So he's burning down the forest."

"Well it's not that bad, of course," I say. "So he gets a bucket and fills it with water from Walden Pond. His cabin's on Walden Pond, right?" Everybody nods. "And he quickly puts out the fire, and there's hardly any damage. And best of all, nobody's there to blame him, or call him out, or fine him, or whatever."

"I don't think you got fined for starting fires, in those days," says Katie, pursing her lips. "They had fires all the time." The table grows suddenly quiet—compared to the rest of the cafeteria—and everybody sort of looks down at the remains of their lunch. I think I'm close to blowing it; these guys are going to think I'm too weird, or just stupid.

"Well, anyway, I'd never write that for class. I'd be going out on a limb, huh? Get it?" I grin. Mild smiles. Better than weird looks, anyway. I stumble forward. "Well, I, uh, used to know a guy who sort of admired what Thoreau was all about, and I guess he talked about this stuff at some point." *Dammit, Peter, wouldja leave me alone? You're not helping here.*

"So, anyway," says Cynthia, changing the subject quickly, "Katie, and Leo and me—"

"Katie, and Leo, and *I*!" shout Leo and Max with great exaggeration.

"Yeah, whatever," says Cynthia, flicking her plastic spoon at them. "Anyway, we're going to the mall on Saturday." She turns her potato chip bag toward me, her black hair swishing slightly as she spoons another mouthful of yogurt. "Wanna come? The sales are supposed to be awesome this weekend."

"Yeah, I guess so. I mean, I want to, sure." Oh, God, Fran. Is it possible to sound any less enthusiastic? Try again. "That's great. Who's gonna drive?" The mall is, I don't know. I'm supposed to like it, I guess. It's like paradise for teens. But I feel sort of defeated there—maybe there are just too many choices. I can never decide what to buy, what goes with what. I don't want to spend the money I've been saving since I was, like, nine, on stupid stuff that's going to go out of style in three months, that I'll just end up shoving to the back of my drawer. I would always get there, and then somehow I want to leave. It's just not that exciting, really. But I wouldn't say that out loud. I figure I've had my strike out for the day, maybe the month, or even the year.

"Who needs a driver? We just take the city bus," Leo says, giving me a puzzled look. "Oh, right, you're new to this gig. How old were we when we started taking the bus to the mall?" Leo asks around.

"Let's see," says Katie. "Must've been sixth grade."

"No, the summer after sixth, before seventh," says Cynthia.

"And last year we invited Max. He's our mascot," Katie smiled, showing him her perfect white teeth.

"I'm not a mascot," says Max. "Well, maybe just a little." He lifts up his "paws" and barks, then pants. Katie shoves a cookie in his mouth.

"Well, that'll be cool," I say. Even though I had a dream about the mall, I haven't actually been there in awhile. Maybe in a couple of years, in fact. Since I was too young—at least, that's what Mom thought—to take the bus by myself. That sounds really weird, huh, that I haven't been to the mall? What kind of self-respecting teenager am I? Don't I care about my appearance? Don't I have to cruise the dimly lit tables in Abercrombie on a regular basis just to keep up? I don't know. Maybe I do. Or should. Anyway, I haven't. I can't any of this say this out loud, either.

"OK, so let's meet at Northern Parkway and Roland Avenue at, what, ten?" says Cynthia. She's good at planning stuff, I've noticed. She always keeps everything moving forward, somehow.

"Oh my God, that is so way too early," says Katie. "Say eleven-thirty."

18

Yo!" booms a voice, and a cafeteria tray drops onto our table. "Hey! Who's got the math homework? I need to check something real quick." It's Jonathan Somebody-or-other. A skinny dude who looks like his head is too small for his torso. And his feet are humongous.

"You mean you want to steal it," Leo laughs. "Check something? Yeah, right. Like, 'I'm just going to check and see if I missed any of the problems,' Leo says in a high, squeaky voice.

"No, really," Jonathan says, his voice croaking in protest. "Some of those function problems—I just need to see something." The bell rings. Lunch is over. Nobody shares homework with Jonathan. There's sort of an unwritten rule—maybe not for everybody, but for some kids—that if you were too lazy or too boneheaded to do the work and figure it out like everybody else, you're out in the cold. I wouldn't share it, anyway, 'cause I'm never sure I've gotten it right, myself.

Mom is pulling into the driveway with Toby just as I get there.

"Whoa, how'd you do that?" There's a big dent at the back of our old blue Subaru wagon, on the right side, and some of the paint is scraped off. Toby hops out quickly.

"I'll tell her, let me tell her!"

Mom just sighs and begins hauling grocery bags out of the car.

"The store was really crowded, see," Toby's practically yelling, "and Mom had to go into the underground lot, the one that gets really crowded. And when she was backing out of her space, she was watching for the other cars so she didn't see the big cement pillar thing behind her and wham!"

"Toby, grab your backpack please," Mom says. "I was hardly even moving. The car must be made out of tinfoil."

"Not Subarus, Mom, they're really strong."

"Well, you're strong too, so take these bags from me so we can do this all in one trip."

19

"Mom, were you really looking?" I ask.

"What kind of question is that? Of course I was looking."

"I mean, were you distracted, or really tired, or—"

"What on earth are you driving at? I was fine. Am fine. Here, now take this." I don't have a good feeling about this, but asking more questions won't get me any answers. So I just let it go. But you can't really let something go that bothers you, once it starts bothering you. I feel this thing, this ball of worry—sort of an orange-y hot thing, I think—settle in the pit of my stomach. This car business. Something's not right. I mean, anybody can have an accident, or a little fender-bender. But this is Mom's second one this year. She's never been the careless type, or spacey. I mean, she goes around the house changing the toilet paper roll in all three bathrooms right before each one runs out. How could anyone keep track of stuff like that? Mom always has. So banging up the car—again. That's not right.

We get inside and Toby lunges for a bag of chips that's sticking out of one of the grocery bags.

"No," says Mom. I notice all of a sudden that he's got big feet, too, like Jonathan. Not that big, of course, but he's starting to get that out-of-proportion look. His feet must be growing a lot faster than his brain.

"But I'm staaarving!" Toby wails.

"Eat a carrot."

"A carrot! That's too little."

"I know," I smile sweetly, burying my worry deep inside, and opening the sliding drawer next to the oven. "Have a granola bar! They're packed with oats and soy and leaves and twigs and—"

"Yecchh."

"All right, enough," says Mom. "Homework." Toby stomps off to log onto the family PC that sits on a shelf in a corner between the kitchen and the breakfast nook—nothing more than a round table with a bench, where Toby and I used to sit making bread balls in the morning on weekends, before my parents were

20

up. Seems like eons ago, but it wasn't really all that long ago. I know he's going to play Slime Ball or one of those race car games until somebody tells him not to. He's only in sixth grade; he doesn't really have that much homework.

"So, Mom, did you sell the house?" I ask, sliding a carrot from the bag on the counter, which my brother rejected.

"What house?" Mom says.

"The one on Keswick you were going to show today."

"Oh, that. Well, we were there for about five minutes this morning, I think. The woman decided right away it was too small. How she's going to find anything bigger in her price range, I don't know."

"Didn't she know the size before you got there?"

"I guess she did, but—I don't know Fran. I can't figure out what people looking for a house are really looking for." Mom rubs her cheek with her shoulder, and shakes back her hair, which I notice is mostly gray, at this point. I think about what she just said: If she, a real estate agent, doesn't know what people buying houses are looking for, why does she do it? This is probably not the best time to pursue this line of thinking. So instead I watch as Mom does, like, four different things at the same time—talking to me, setting up water to boil for spaghetti, unpacking three bags of groceries, and emptying the dishwasher. And I stand there doing nothing. I guess I'm waiting to be asked. She's OK, I decide.

"Why are you giving me that strange look?" Mom asks, opening a jar of spaghetti sauce. "Is my hair crooked? Did I grow horns without noticing?"

"I'm not. I just, I don't know."

"Well, why don't you set the table and then hit the books. Your father should be home in about half an hour." I shrug and begin pulling silverware out of the drawer. Minutes later, as I begin heading upstairs, I turn to see my mother standing at the counter, still as a statute, her hands flat on the countertop, as if for support. It's a vision I want to shake off, but I can't. One more thing to shove into that closet of mine, where the darkness covers up everything you can't bear to look at up close.

English 9-2
P. Richards
10/20/07

Life on Walden Pond
By Fran Singer

My garden is coming along nicely. The peas have risen to the top of the wooden stakes I planted, the corn is nearly up to my shoulder, and the potatoes will be ready to harvest next month. I believe I shall have enough produce to sell, so I can buy sufficient supplies of tinned meats and candles for the winter. But the main thing is, I am alone. So alone that when I sit still in my cabin, I can hear my own breath drawing in and out. I can hear a woodchuck in the forest, as his paws crackle over dry twigs and leaves. This is freedom, I think. To be alone like this. No one to tell me what to do. No laws to obey. No responsibility for anyone else. I am mistake-free. I cannot go wrong—I cannot do wrong. And even if I did, no one would have to know about it.

I wrote earlier this week in my journal that a man is rich only "in proportion to the number of things he can afford to let alone." I believe what I meant by that was that people don't need possessions to be happy. I would add now, on reflection, that it isn't just "things" people need to let alone in order to find true happiness. There are things you cannot see or touch that you have to learn to let go of, too, or they will keep weighing you down, like the possessions I watched being sold at auction recently. These things are ideas, or visions in your head. And it's not nearly as easy to get rid of them as a bunch of old pots and pans. Maybe while I'm out here, alone in the woods, I can work on that—on letting go of the things, the ideas, I don't need anymore, or don't want to keep. Maybe that's the way to find happiness.

Chapter 3

The cup is so hot I don't think I can hold it. Cynthia grabs a brown cardboard sleeve and slides it on for me. Better. At least the heat's less intense. I bring the cup to my lips and cautiously take a sip. At first, all I taste is whipped cream that's melting and sort of hot and cold together. Then a liquid that's chocolatey and minty and also sort of dark and bitter.

"Well?" They're all watching me intently—Cynthia, Katie, Leo, and Max—like I'm some sort of alien who's just landed on earth and is having her first experience on a foreign planet. I can't disappoint them. Actually, I realize, I don't really have the luxury of not liking this. I think I'm required to like it. To love it. So I decide there and then that I do. I figure that's a pretty small price to pay to begin having friends again.

"Mmmm," I say. "Starbucks. Where have you been all my life?" The group laughs. It's weird how this one little thing makes me feel like they're really starting to accept me—or maybe trust me. Maybe that's the same thing. Anyway, Cynthia ordered for me. A tall mint mocha with whip. Decaf, of course. When we got to the mall, I thought there'd be a long discussion about which stores to hit first. But apparently a decision had already been made—or maybe not made, but assumed, by everyone but me. The first stop would be the Starbucks on the fourth floor. Of course. No brainer. You don't shop until you've caffed up, or at least come close.

"Ladies," says Max, gulping a venti caramel Frappuccino. There's a ribbon of whipped cream on his upper lip. If this were a movie, you'd hear a voice-over saying something like, 'I wanted to kiss away the foam.' But really, that's the last thing I want to do in this situation. Max is nice; he's even sort of cute in a Charlie Brown kind of way. But I just hand him a napkin; he takes the hint.

"I'm going down to Record and Tape Traders. Then the Apple store. Should we synchronize watches for lunch?"

Just how long are we going to be here, I wonder. Is this an all-day thing? Anyone care for a game of touch football out on the crisp fall leaves, in the park next to the elementary school? Better bide my time on that one. I'm not sure this is a touch football kind of crowd.

"Right," says Cynthia, staring down at her orange Swatch. "We need some time. So how about one-thirty, in front of the bakery in the food court? Call my cell if you're going to be late. We'll do the same." The others nod. "OK, Max, shoo."

"Byyyee," Katie calls out, giving him a little wave. "Don't spend all your money. Save some for meee!" Max offers a lopsided grin and shuffles off.

"And now," says Leo, throwing away her empty Starbucks cup. "The moment we've all been waiting for." Cynthia puts her hands on my shoulders.

"We want to help you with your look," Cynthia says. She grips my shoulders hard. "Now don't take this the wrong way. We like you. We really do. That's why we want to help you bring out your feminine side a bit more."

"You're really attractive," Leo adds. "I'm not a lesbian or anything. But everyone can see that you're pretty. But you sort of walk around like you're trying to hide—"

"She means you wear such baggy clothes all the time," says Katie. "Like, those khakis and that sweatshirt you're wearing now. They're Gap, and that's good. That's cool. But when was the last time you wore a skirt, Fran?"

I can feel my face turning red all the way to the base of my neck. My ears are burning. I don't know if I can handle this—all the attention, the touching. When I was younger, I loved being the center of attention. But not now, not now. I'm not ready for any close-ups.

"Gee," I say softly. "I really appreciate…I'm not, uh, sure this…I mean, I'm really OK with…."

24

"Oh, don't thank us now. Wait until we put together your new look," says Katie.

"I think she just needs some space, guys," says Cynthia.

"So how much money did you bring?" asks Leo, releasing her grip on my shoulders. "We've only got an hour or so before we have to meet Max for lunch." Well, I think, at least they waited until Max was out of sight before embarrassing me half to death.

"Hmmm. That one. I like that one best." Cynthia is sitting cross-legged on my bed, hugging my rainbow-colored peace pillow. She eyes the outfit I've got on—the fourth one I've tried, I think. I'm wearing a skirt for the first time in ages and ages. Courtesy of my personal makeover team. The tag's still attached— just in case. It feels sort of funny—I mean, I feel exposed. The skirt is so short I can feel the air moving up inside my legs. But that doesn't really bother me. It's just the, well, the *skirtness* of it. "I love the way that paisley print looks on you," Cynthia says. "It goes really well with your skin coloring. And that top—really sweet." The blouse is loose and sort of peasanty, gauzy. It's light and airy. You can just see my bra through it. The sort of thing a girl would wear who wants to be noticed—and to let people know she really doesn't have a care in the world. How could I possibly be that girl?

"I'm freezing," I complain, hugging my arms.

"Oh, no you're not. And besides, it's worth it. You look really great. Let's try putting your hair up. See how that works." Cynthia slides off my bed in search of a brush, comb, and various hairclips, which sit in a basket on top of my dresser. "You know, this room reminds me of something. You know that movie, where the little girl is at a boarding school where the headmistress treats her really well only because she's rich, and when she loses her money—I forget how—she's sent up to the attic to live with the servant. Do you know that one?"

I smile. "It's *The Little Princess*. Used to be one of my favorite books."

"That's right! That's right!" Cynthia's green eyes widen. "I remember now. It was one of my favorites, too. I love that part where the monkey climbs across the buildings into the girls' room—"

"—and they wake up and see all that food that miraculously appeared, after they're half-starved for weeks," I smile.

"Anyway, this room sort of reminds me of that attic. I mean, it's not shaped like an attic. But even though you don't have a lot of stuff in here—you should see my room, talk about cluttered—it's all sort of cozy. Like you could just curl up here with the pillow—" she grabs the peace pillow off the bed... "and sit here in the windowsill..." she sits in my favorite spot, the built-in bench that's right beneath my window, which looks out at a giant maple tree. The tree is almost bare now, but a few orange leaves still cling to the branches. The window seat is covered with a blue and gold fabric filled with moons and stars. I remember picking it out with my dad at a remnant store. I must have been in fifth grade. The year I decided I was too old for pink unicorns—the prevailing theme of my bedroom, up to that point. My dad is a well-rounded sort of guy—he likes designs, and colors, and figuring out how things go together in a room. I guess it's related to the kind of work he does, helping buildings rise up out of nothing. "You could just, I don't know, daydream for a long time," Cynthia continues.

"I know just what you mean. Exactly. I've done that." And to think that I was worried about inviting Cynthia up here. What's the big deal? It's just a bedroom, for God's sake, and anyway, she feels comfortable here. That's the important thing. After all, the walls can't speak. The thoughts that have filled this room—filled it so full the room itself felt like a giant, thin-skinned balloon ready to pop, and I along with it—Cynthia can't touch that, smell it, or taste it. To her, it's just some girl's bedroom.

26

"Music!" Cynthia exclaims. "We need inspiration!" I click on iTunes on the Mac sitting on my desk, and let Cynthia scroll through my playlist. I haven't added anything in awhile, but I'm pretty sure she'll find something to play among the 213 songs already on there. That's not a huge selection, of course, but it's a start. I remind myself to start buying tunes again. Before she can click on a song, I reach over and do it first.

The things that I've loved, things that I've lost
Things I've held sacred that I've dropped
I won't lie no more you can bet
I don't want to learn what I'll need to forget

"Interesting choice," says Cynthia. I watch for her reaction as she stands quietly for a moment, nodding to the music. "Audioslave?" I nod. "I don't have anything of theirs. Kind of makes you think, doesn't it?" I nod again. "Stand there," she says, "in front of the mirror. I'm going to try an up-do." Cynthia sweeps a hunk of my heavy brown hair in her hands and begins thrusting combs and clips in all directions to hold the mess up. The feel of someone else's hands on my hair has a strange, calming effect. I stand in front of the mirror that's screwed into my closet door, close my eyes, and sway gently, letting Cynthia's busy hands and the steady thrum of music lull me into a sort of trance. I remember this feeling…from a time before…when I was younger and everything I saw or touched or smelled or tasted was simple, uncomplicated. Little things could make me so happy then—it was so easy to do. Honey drizzled on warm toast. The smell of summer peaches ripening in a bowl, running in and out of the sprinkler in the back yard on a hot day, Toby dodging drops, running around on his chubby little baby legs, laughing and squealing wildly. And Mom knotting my long braid at night after a bath. Her fingers, gentle and firm like Cynthia's, taming my hair one loop at a time, until I felt so sleepy, my head would begin to tip over. Mom would kiss my neck gently, and half-carry, half-walk me to bed. This bed, in this room. But it was a different room, too. Another time and place. And it was covered in unicorns.

"Well, would you look at that," Cynthia says, breaking into my daydream. "I don't think I need to go to college. I'm just gonna open up a beauty shop, like Queen Latifah in that movie, and create works of art out of women's hair." Cynthia smiles in that way I'm learning to recognize—her green eyes crinkling, her shiny black hair swinging as she shakes her head in amusement.

"I don't know if I'll come," I say, watching for her reaction in the mirror.

"What do you mean, you won't come? 'Course you will." She plucks at the loose strands of hair that frame my face, arranging them somehow, so they look even more natural.

"Well, I may decide to shave off all my hair before that, try the bald look for awhile."

"You wouldn't ever. Just look at you. It works." I turn my head slowly from side to side, holding my own gaze in the mirror. Yeah, I guess it works.

"So, your first dance at Westmore. Don't get too excited. Nothing much happens and the music is really crappy sometimes. One time, I guess it was in seventh grade, Katie, and Leo, and me—and *I*—anyway, we were standing at the side of the gym laughing the whole time. The music was just so bad and everybody looked so unbelievably dorky dancing."

"Are you gonna dance?" I ask. "This time, I mean." To say I have mixed feelings about this is an understatement. I'm not a total shrinking violet—but I desperately don't want to look like a dork, either.

"Depends," Cynthia shrugs. "You?"

"Depends," I reply, pulling the combs out of my hair, and giving it a shake.

Chapter 4

Friday comes, as it always does, at the end of a week where I've spent every waking moment trying not to screw up, trying not to give my inner demons room to breathe, trying not to flunk a test, and trying desperately but invisibly to prove once and for all that Cynthia, Leo, and the others have not been wasting their time on me. No wonder I'm so tired. But it's Friday night, the night of the Westmore Senior Fall Fest Dance (the lamest name ever, but I'm not sure who's to blame). Guess how I'm getting there? I could have gotten a ride with Max's older brother Tom, who's a junior. He's taking his girlfriend, Amber, and Katie and Troke and some other kids I don't really know. But no, that's not happening. I sort of wanted to ride with them, but when Cynthia and Leo found out that my dad drove a big bright red pickup, they decided that would be way more fun. Riding in the back of an open pickup in November, wearing a camisole and a miniskirt?

"No, that's cool," said Leo, as we headed down the corridor to American History class. "I'll bring a blanket. And we can stretch out and wave our arms and stuff."

"It's not a parade float, Leo, it's just a stupid truck," I say. "I don't know what stuff he's got back there. Maybe tools and stuff. It's probably dirty."

"I'm sure he'll clean it out for us, won't he?" Actually, he would. In fact, I already knew for a fact that my dad would not let a herd of stampeding buffaloes stop him from a chance to drive me and my friends to a party. I could already picture his expression when I tell him he's been anointed. Thank God he's not chaperoning. It's drop and run, for sure.

Friday afternoon, right after last period, Leo and I found Cynthia at her locker. "Guess how we're getting to the dance tonight?" Leo asks.

"Oh, God, I don't know. Should I ask my mother to drop me off a block away from school? What do you think? Ugghh, I can't wait to get my license."

"We're riding in Fran's dad's pickup truck."

"We are?" Cynthia said. She nodded slowly. "OK, I guess that's cool."

"It wasn't my idea," I add hastily. "But I know he'll do it. You sure you don't mind riding in a truck?"

"No, no, it'll be great. It's so much less predictable than pulling up in a stupid minivan. By the way, Leo, have you seen Fran's dad?"

"No, why?" Leo asked, bundling notebooks into her backpack. The teachers have really been packing us with homework for this last quarter. Sunday is going to be all about memorizing the table of periodic elements and reading up on the Civil War.

"He's a dish," Cynthia grins.

"Eww," I blurt. "How can you say that? My dad? He's, so, I don't know, weird. And he limps. Did you notice that?"

"He's not weird. And no, I didn't notice a limp. I think you're exaggerating, Fran," says Cynthia. "He's really cute—for an older guy. I can see why your mother fell for him. He's sort of sweet, with his hair all long and curling on the back of his shirt." Cynthia had only met my dad for, like, five minutes after he came home, on the day she was in my room helping me try on clothes. I had no idea she paid such close attention.

"He just needs a haircut," I say. "He's always forgetting and letting his hair get too long so that it sticks up all over his head. That is *not* cute!"

"Anyway, it'll be fun riding in the pickup," Cynthia says.

"After that build-up, I am *so* looking forward to meeting this dreamy Mr. Singer," says Leo in an exaggerated tone, crossing her arms over her heart and looking skyward.

"Oh, God," I say. But despite my embarrassment—and hearing them talk that way about my dad is about the most

30

disgusting thing I can think of—I'm secretly pleased. One more notch of approval, or acceptance, or whatever you want to call it, on my belt. Little by little, I'm becoming human again. And my IM list? Better. Not respectable yet, but better.

The pickup pulls up outside the long brick front of Westmore. Dad leaps out and unlatches the door at the back of the truck bed, then offers an arm to each of us. Navigating the four feet down to the ground isn't easy in heels and a tight skirt.

"Thank you, Mr. Singer," say Leo and Cynthia, with just the merest hint of flirtation in their voices.

"Ladies, have a nice evening. I'll pull up at eleven for the return trip. Everybody OK with that?" asks Dad, playing the gentleman to the hilt. I know he's enjoying himself immensely. "Have a great time tonight. Don't do anything I wouldn't do." We burst out laughing. Does he really know what high school kids get up to, these days?

"Bye, Dad," I murmur, moving away from the truck as quickly as my heels will carry me. Despite the cold November air, loads of kids are milling around outside. I suspect many of them are dying for a cancer stick, but several teachers are out here acting as chaperones, including Christa Neal, my House guardian and keeper of law and order. So for one more night, anyway, some young lungs are protected from turning to black ash. Neal sees me and flashes an enormous grin. I'm sorry, but she just looks goofy standing out here in her ankle-high black boots with furry grey trim around the tops.

"Hi, Fran!" Christa Neal shouts across the crowd to me. "Have a great time tonight! Don't freeze out here! Don't you look adorable!" Is it my imagination, or does she actually wink at me? Where do the schools find these people, anyway? Cynthia and Leo appear at my side. Neal is so far beneath their notice, they don't even see her waving wildly.

"Let's get inside, I'm freezing," says Cynthia.

"Oh, you're the one who said we wouldn't be cold," I say. "I think even my shoulders are numb, so come on!"

A wall of warm, moist air hits us as we step inside. The music coming from the gym down the hall is so loud, you can feel the linoleum floor vibrating. Even the air seems to be vibrating. Several parents and teachers are perched at tables blocking our path to the gym. We have to get our hands stamped before we go in. It's a crowd control thing; like we're a bunch of cattle that need tagging.

"I can't stand getting ink on my hand," Leo whispers as we angle past the tables. "Let's go to the bathroom and wash it off before we get all sweaty in the gym." So we do. Personally, I don't care about a circle of ink on the back of my hand. It really doesn't bother me. But Leo is, I'd guess you'd say, fastidious. Never gets crumbs on her jeans at lunch. Never even has a zit, come to think of it.

When we finally step out into the gym, the music is so loud, it's practically solid. Two people—one boy, one girl, both in their late teens, probably—are fiddling with a digital console that controls the music. Huge speakers are placed in each corner of the room, the connecting wires all flattened down on the gym floor with black electrical tape. Some techno piece I don't recognize is blaring. The floor is packed with Westmore kids dancing—if you can call what they do dancing. Looks more like boxing to me—weaving, bobbing, circling around, and stomping. The lights in the gym are dim, and I can smell the heat and sweat rising off of all the bodies in the room. Since it's too loud to talk, Cynthia grabs me by the wrist and pulls me toward the wall under the basketball hoop. She leans into my ear and I can smell her lavender perfume.

"Look, there's Max with Katie. Don't you think they're cute together?" I follow her gaze to the middle of the floor, where Max and Katie are grinding away, next to each other, but not touching. A few feet away from them there's a tall guy I don't recognize. He's got broad shoulders and light brown wavy hair. I don't know why he catches my eye in this roomful of people; there's nothing special about him. But anyway, he does.

"Who's that?" I ask Cynthia, my lips practically grazing her ear as I point directly toward Broad Shoulders. There's so much going on in here, no one's going to notice the pointing. Cynthia looks at me with an amused smile.

"Carter Brown. Known him since kindergarten. He used to be a skinny little shrimp, can you believe it?" Usher is playing now, and I start bouncing a little to the beat. "Do you want me to—"

"No, no, God, no," I say quickly. "Just wondering. He's just, I don't know. He looks OK, I guess."

"He is. He's basically really normal. Kind of boring, actually. Quiet, too. When we were little, he was really into dinosaurs. Typical, huh?"

"Hey." Leo pops up next to us, and other girl is with her. Leo looks about five years older tonight, probably because of her outfit: a shimmery ivory camisole with a midriff one-button sweater over it and a slinky brown miniskirt and pink heels. The pink heels are a bit much, I think, but OK, that's her style and she pulls it off. She's got stockings on, too, and they also seem to shimmer. "Didja see Max and Katie? Cute, huh?"

"We saw. We liked," says Cynthia, practically screaming to be heard above the music. Usher has morphed into Darude's Sandstorm.

"Fran, do you know Sabina?" Leo shouts. Sabina looks vaguely familiar, but I don't know her. We exchange brief smiles.

"Hi," says Sabina distractedly. "Hmm, I spy with my little eye…Carter Brown. Think I'll mosey onto the dance floor." Cynthia shoots me a quick glance; I pretend I don't see it. The night flashes by, faster than I expect. After awhile, I dance, sort of, but not with anybody in particular. Once in a while, I sort of glance sideways to see what Carter Brown is up to. Dancing with Sabina, not surprisingly. I'll probably never actually meet the guy—he's a sophomore, anyway. Doesn't matter. At my old school, I probably would've been all over the place, not thinking about much of anything. But I was younger and stupider, and anyway, that was then, this is now.

Chapter 5

The paper fall foliage was bad enough. But a turkey and a pumpkin? On a wall in my locker hallway, someone has actually put up "Thanksgiving decoration." Katie and I stand there staring at it, like it's some sort of holy shrine.

"I don't know, I think it's sort of cute," Katie says, cocking her blonde curls to one side. "Reminds me of when I was little, my mom always bought these little candles for the Thanksgiving table, little Pilgrims—one boy, one girl. The boy Pilgrim wore a black hat and the wick stood up out of the middle. The girl had on a white cap, I think. She had a wick sticking out of her head, too."

"I bet Neal did this," I say. It's close to House, and I wouldn't put it past her. "Maybe she's a thwarted elementary school teacher. You know, she desperately wanted to teach seven year-olds, but for some reason, no one would hire her." Katie yawns and the bell rings.

"Mmm, maybe," she says. "But anyway, I sort of like it,"

I head for Spanish class. *No me gusto los,* uh, lame holiday decorations, I think to myself. A few minutes later, Max is leaning over, whispering to me. "*Señorita! Did you see the sign-up sheet?*

"*Que?*" I whisper back.

"El sign-up sheet, outside the *cafeteria,*" he whispers.

"*Por que?*"

"*La playa,*" Max whispers. "No, wait a minute, *playa* means beach. The play. The ninth grade production. The Really Big Sheeww," he says.

"Señor Luchow," says Señor Guzman, our big, hulking Spanish teacher, addressing Max loudly. "Would you please combine the verbs *estar, ser,* and *hacer* in a sentence for us, please? Come up and write your sentence on the board. *Gracias.*"

And that was the end of that conversation. I dimly recall Christa Neal announcing something about the play sign-up sheet a few days ago—a day or two after the dance, I think. But it didn't really register because Cynthia and I were deep in conversation about Sabina and Carter and their bump-and-grind act at the dance. For the record, I did not start this conversation, Cynthia did. I'm not gonna fish for information. I've got my pride—or at least, I'm working on getting some.

"Anyway, she's sort of a tramp," Cynthia said, while Neal blabbed the announcements for the week.

"That's harsh," I replied.

"No, not really. She's had this pattern since sixth grade—you don't know her. She just throws herself at some guy and sort of demands a physical response. She forces them to touch her."

"That's so—"

"Yeah, exactly," said Cynthia. "That's why I used the 'T' word. And when she gets bored, she moves on to the next victim."

"Well, the guys have something to do with this—"

"Yeah, but she always seems to start it. Take Carter. He hasn't been going with anyone. I'm not really sure he's interested. Between you and me—" Cynthia leans in across the table and lowers her voice to a stage whisper—"I think Carter might be gay. And if he is, he's definitely not out, not even to me." I think about this for a moment. How can you tell? Why did he catch my eye at the dance? If he were gay, wouldn't I have picked up some sort of vibe?

"But you said they were all over each other," I said.

"Yeah, but you know, people do things for show. Carter likes to be liked. He doesn't want to send a signal to everybody that he's off-limits, if you know what I mean," Cynthia replied. Our conversation was cut short by the bell, yet again.

That night, after practically drooling on my math text book because I was so tired, I tossed in bed for a long time, unable to fall asleep. When I finally fell asleep—I refused to look at the clock, to see how late it was—I had a long, complicated dream in which Peter was teaching Carter Brown how to communicate with dolphins, using a special language involving clicks, and squeaks, and all sorts of weird noises. They were standing at the edge of a huge sunny pool filled with dolphins leaping about, like the Dolphin Vista tourist trap we visited in Miami several years ago. I was watching them, but they didn't see me. All of a sudden, Carter jumped into the pool and started swimming with the dolphins. Soon he was leaping out of the water, his body arched and graceful, just like the dolphins, his wavy hair wet and flowing behind him. Peter stood there watching, a big smile on his face. "You're learning," he said. "That's good. Now keep it going."

Chapter 6

Toby is pouring milk onto his chocolate Cocoa Puffs and it's spilling all over the table. "Dad," he says, leaning down to slurp the milk off the kitchen table. "Are we having Thanksgiving this year?"

"Where have you been?" I ask, shoving books into my backpack. "We always have Thanksgiving."

"I thought, if Mom's not feeling well…"

"Who said anything about your mother not feeling well?" Dad asks. He's already got his coat on, ready to run out the door to wherever there's a building he's got to babysit. "Toby?"

"She seems kind of tired," Toby said, slurping Cocoa Puffs. "I thought maybe we'd go out to dinner instead, so she doesn't have to cook. You know, a restaurant could be fun." This conversation is made possible by the fact that my mother, usually the first one down in the kitchen, is in fact not down yet. I glance nervously toward the back stairs, to see if she's on her way.

'Why isn't she down, Dad?" I ask. Dad puts down his briefcase and sits on a kitchen stool. He's still got his coat on. "I don't know, exactly. She told me last night she was very tired. I guess she's just sleeping in. She's entitled once in awhile, isn't she?" Dad asks, trying to make it seem like this is a normal everyday thing for Mom—which it isn't.

"That's why we should go out for Thanksgiving," Toby says. "You know, like on that commercial where everybody surprises the mom by announcing they're all going to Burger King, or something."

"Hmm, that's very considerate of you, Tobe," Dad says. "But it's too late. Uncle Henry, Aunt Syl, my father, your cousins—they're all coming here. Everything's going to be just like normal." Now, "normal" has become a very loaded word in

38

my family. So when Dad says everything's going to be "normal," well, that's when I really start to worry.

"I'm going to go up and say goodbye to Mom," I say.

"Me, too," says Toby. We both glance at Dad for a second. He hesitates, but then says we should go ahead. We tiptoe up the backstairs and down the hallway to our parents' bedroom.

"Mom?" I whisper. She's got the blanket pulled up over her head, but she stirs.

"Hmm? Sweetie, what is it?" she asks, her voice muffled by the covers.

"We gotta leave for school, Mom" Toby whispers hoarsely. "Are you sick?"

"No, honey. I'm fine." She sits up and rubs her eyes. Her hair is sticking up in odd clumps around her head.

"Well, we gotta go, or we'll miss the bus," I say. "We just wanted to make sure you were all right."

"Of course I'm all right. I'm just tired," she says.

"Come on, Tobe, we gotta go. See you this afternoon, Mom. Actually, I'll be late. Tryouts."

"Tryouts? Like for a team?" asks Toby.

"Something," I mumble, turning away, and hoping Mom's still too sleepy to start asking questions.

"Like what? Girl's basketball?" asks Toby, his voice rising. "It's too late for field hockey. Mom, I'm definitely gonna try out for baseball in the spring. Just thought you should know. And Sam told me he's gonna go to baseball camp in the summer, and I wanted to ask you if I could go with him—"

"Toby?" I say sternly. "Could you possibly shut up and let Mom go back to sleep?"

"No, no, it's OK," Mom says, sitting up. She manages a crooked smile. "I guess I'm awake now," but she still looks puffy and groggy, I think.

"Come on, Tobe, we gotta go."

"Bye, Mom," he says. I can see he's thinking about leaning over to kiss her, but he doesn't. So she's tired, so what? I'm tired a

39

lot, and there's nothing wrong with me—well, not technically, anyway. It's probably just one of those mid-life things women go through. That's it, I think. It's just menopause. A normal life event. A normal, everyday occurrence.

Thoughts of Mom float in the back of my head all day in school. I feel like I'm drifting in and out of some sort of dream. Was she OK? Of course she's OK. She's Mom. She's always OK. Even through the awful times, she's always been right there—present, whole, sane. When I'd be hysterical, she'd be right there beside me, calm, maybe even Buddha-like. So why the new act now? Tired instead of energetic. Staring off into space at odd moments. There are puffy bags under her eyes, I noticed. Maybe just the "ravages of age," as they say. But she's only 47. That's not very old.

In chemistry class, we're told to do a lab experiment—something about chromatography. You're supposed to sort different liquids through a glass tube and then watch them separate depending on how thick they are, or something—I think the word the teacher used is *viscous*. Sounds like *vicious* to me. Vicious liquids. My lab partner, a guy named Tim Armstrong, keeps reaching across me to get something or other. He has really bad breath and I think he's trying to look down my bra. That breaks through my dream state, all right. I tell him to move over because I'm cramped—he's in my space!—and he does. He doesn't say much. Just breathes out his foul breath, mostly. The lab is boring because we don't get to mix any interesting chemicals and watch them change colors. That's my favorite thing to do in chem lab. Instead, we just watched these smelly solvents and things dribble down and separate in the tube column. Whoop-dee-doo. Everybody's scribbling in their lab notebooks, trying to look interested. Maybe some of them are, I don't know. Not Troke, that's for sure. He could care less. He's over at the next table, his long hair falling like a greasy brown curtain over his face. Good thing we're not using Bunsen burners today; he'd go up in flames. Anyway, Troke's snorting through his nose—a stifled laugh.

40

Maybe he'd be more fun to have as a lab partner than Tim Stink. Anyway, I have this silly thought, as I half-heartedly jot down observations in my lab notebook, which is full of intricate drawings and equations. As if I really knew what I was doing. Anyway, if I could get hold of the right chemicals, right here in the lab, maybe I could mix up some sort of potion that would help Mom feel like her old self. Or maybe I could invent a potion that would help you get rid of certain memories—sort of like cleanser for your brain. *Mr. Clean removes even the stubbornest stains!* Stupid, I know. I've already seen that sci-fi flick. It never works out. Forget it, I tell myself.

I try to shake off my mood—and keep Tim Armstrong out of my way. The minute the bell rings, I grab my books and walk out of the science room without a backward glance. I catch up with Leo in the hallway, which echoes loudly with the sound of lockers slamming as people jam their books in.

"Hey," I say. "What are you doing for Thanksgiving?"

"Driving to New Jersey," Leo says drily.

"You sound less than thrilled. Relatives? Boring cousins?"

"Yeah, and a mean uncle and my grandparents, who act like it's still 1944 or something. They're always like, 'Have a cookie, honey, you're a growing girl, you need to keep up your strength,' or 'Is that what your mother lets you wear to school? You mean you're permitted to wear those open-toed sandals? Oh my!' They act like they've never seen flip-flops. Plus, my grandmother can't cook to save her life, so the turkey's usually really dry and the gravy tastes like starch. The whole thing is such an ordeal." Leo slams her locker. "Hey," she says, raising her eyebrows mischievously, "maybe I could just go to your Thanksgiving instead. Ya think?"

"Oh, you'd have a blast," I reply. "My Aunt Syl is nuts. I mean, really nuts. She likes to pretend she's a fortune teller. She calls me and my brother into the den, or somewhere dark, and wraps a kerchief around her head, and says she can see the future."

"Whoa, that's weird. Sorry, she's your aunt and all."

41

"Yeah, and my father's dad is blind, so we have to lead him around everywhere. It's 'cause of his diabetes. And my grandmother is deaf, so we're always shouting. Sure, come to my house. It'll be great." I walk away from my locker empty-handed, but Leo's carrying a book.

"What's that?"

"*Lord of the Flies.*"

"Oh, right, we're supposed to read that in the next couple of weeks, aren't we?" I ask, wanting to forget all about homework, for awhile.

"Actually, I already started it," Leo says. "It's really cool. These three English boys are stuck on a deserted island, and one of them is called Piggy."

"It sounds funny. Why would we get to read a funny book?"

"It is funny, sort of," Leo says. "But you know how you can tell in a book, some times, that something's going to go wrong? How you just sort of get this feeling?"

"Yeah, I guess," I say. My experience with things going wrong doesn't really come from books, but there's no point in bringing that up.

"That's what this book feels like. But I don't know. I haven't gotten very far yet."

Some people might think Leo is sort of dorky for being both really smart and super-organized. But deep down, I wish I were more like her. She seems so together all the time—always in control. No surprises. Like she's able to get a handle on things, even before they happen. But that's ridiculous—things can happen really quickly that you can't control. And then there's no time to figure out how to handle it.

"Guess I'll start it next week," I say. "I gotta concentrate on just getting through Thanksgiving." Leo laughs.

Leo and I walk slowly down the corridor, not speaking. I guess we're both thinking about how we're going to survive the holiday and keep our sanity. Also I'm thinking about Mom again—and how she's going to cope with it all, this year. Usually, it's no big deal for her. She always seems to like taking charge of the whole event, getting Grandpa Alex—her father-in-law—comfortably seated and out of mischief. Getting the turkey on the table at four-thirty p.m. on the dot. But can she pull it off this year? I can't think why not—yet for the first time, I'm wondering. I stop walking when we reach the hall near the main entrance—one of those places where someone put up brown-and-orange paper turkeys.

"Aren't you coming out to catch the bus?" Leo asks.

"Um, I just realized I forgot some stuff in my locker. My sweatpants are in there—and they reek. I'd better bring 'em home."

"OK. Well, good luck with the turkey thing."

"You, too." Lying is so easy, it's scary. You can just say the first believable thing that pops into your head, and people just accept it. Maybe I should lie more often; it sure is easier than telling the truth. A whole lot easier. Anyway, there are no dirty sweatpants in my locker. Today, Wednesday—the day before Thanksgiving—is the ninth grade play tryouts. At my old school, nobody would ever schedule an activity the day before a major holiday, but what do I know. Maybe it's a test to find out if anybody's really interested. I'm not even sure how I'm going to get home. But anyway, this audition thing—I didn't tell my friends, not Cynthia, not Leo. I don't think they're into the whole drama thing. I mean, Cynthia loves to dissect people's personalities, and Leo loves reading about all sorts of stuff. But the stage—I don't know, I think it's too fake for them.

People wander into the auditorium in slow motion, almost shuffling, heads down. I get it: Everybody wants to look ultra-casual. Like who really cares about being in a play, right? But if they didn't care, why did they come, when they could be hanging at Starbucks, licking the whipped cream off the top of a Frappuccino? Now take me. I don't really know why I'm bothering. The drama teacher doesn't know me. Nobody knows I used to do a lot of school theater. Even went to theater camp for a couple of summers. That's one I'm keeping to myself. The last thing I want is to be labeled as a drama geek before I've even had a chance to figure this place out. And even if I got a part—let's say, a big part—in this play, I'm not at all sure I'm ready for the pressure. The spotlight. Too much about *me*. I'm trying to take a vacation from *me*, for awhile—or at least, the old me.

So I take a seat at the very back of the auditorium, in a seat far away from everyone else—as close to the door as possible. But Max finds me and plops down next to me.

"So, *Signorita*, you're putting your life on the line, huh?" Something like that, I think.

"Well, you know. . ."

"Yeah, well, I sort of had fun last year. We did *Inherit the Wind*. I played Matthew Brady, the super-religious guy who doesn't think evolution should be taught in schools. You weren't here, right?" The thing about Max is, even when he talks like this, you still like the guy. He doesn't sound stuck-up or conceited, or full of himself. He just sounds like he's telling you something that might or might not interest you, and he doesn't really care one way or the other. It's like this was all something that just happened to him in an amusing sort of way, and now he's passing it on.

"Cool," I nod. I know the play he's talking about. He had the lead role. But he doesn't put it that way. That's Max for you. Still, there's no way I'm going to tell him the Helen Keller story. "So what's the director like?" The director is the high school drama teacher, Bill Kirby.

"He's, um, not what you might expect. He's sort of like a drill sergeant. A no-nonsense type of guy. I think he probably should've joined the Navy, or something. He's a real hard-ass."

"Is that good or bad?" I ask, eyeing Max. He drapes his long legs over the back of the seat in front of him, and slouches down. Max always seems ultra-relaxed. But nobody can be relaxed all the time, can they? I hardly know the meaning of the word, myself."Good, I think. Because he really tries to make everybody

44

do the best they can. Which is what you want when you're up on stage acting like an idiot," Max smiles.

Bill Kirby strides to the center of the stage, right into a spotlight. You gotta wonder what type of guy would plan this out. Setting up a spotlight for himself.

"OK, people, listen up!" he says, in a booming stage voice. Max is right: This guy's got military written all over him. He reminds me of those drill sergeants in the movies, who are always yelling at the young recruits at the top of their lungs, telling them to shape up or ship out. He's even got the hair for it—practically a crew-cut. "As you know, this year we're doing *Romeo and Juliet.*" Loud whispering immediately fills the auditorium. This must be Kirby's sense of humor. The tradition at Westmore, I have already learned, is that nobody knows what play will be chosen before the first day of tryouts. Maybe Kirby thinks more people will come to audition if they can't prejudge. So this is news for everybody.

Max leans over to me. "This could be a disaster," he says. "Shakespeare," he adds, shaking his head.

"It works like this," Mr. Kirby says. "One. Everybody comes down here and picks up a script. Two. I'm going to call you up on stage, in pairs, from the sign-up list. Three. I'll tell you which pages to read from. Four. I'll tell you when to stop reading. And when I say 'stop,' ladies and gentlemen, I do mean stop." At this, laughter ripples through the audience. "Any questions? Oh, if we don't finish today by five, I'll hear the rest of you on Monday, after Thanksgiving break. Unless you change your mind, of course, between now and then. In which case, I'll just cross you off the list. It's no skin off my nose. Now, any questions?"

Several things are going through my mind at once. Do I want any part of this? If I get up there and read, and I stumble over all those weird Elizabethan words, am I gonna hate myself? This guy Kirby must really enjoy embarrassing us, since he doesn't want to give anybody any prep time. No carefully rehearsed monologues. Those are the easy questions. There's more, welling up in my stomach like a sour fireball: Do I even deserve to try?

45

Am I worth it? Getting it, I mean. If I get it, is that a sign that it's OK for me go ahead and live my life—to attract good karma?

"Fran?. . . Fran?" I turn to Max, still sitting next to me. "Are you OK? You're hunched over there like you're gonna hurl. Does Shakespeare always have that effect on you?"

"Oh, I'm fine. I'm, I don't know, it's fine. So," I add quickly, "you ready to get up there?"

"Oh, yeah, sure. Whatever. I mean, what's the worst that could happen? So I'll sound like an idiot. I won't be the only one. Only I hope he doesn't call me up to read with Sabina."

"Oh, is she here?" I ask, temporarily forgetting my own panic. I scan the rows in front of us. And sure enough, there's Sabina way down front. And next to her—who else?—Carter Brown. Since he's a sophomore, he can't try out. So maybe he's there to give her moral support. Gee, Cynthia was right. She *does* work fast. "Why? Isn't she any good?"

"Oh, God. She's like the worst. Every time she reads something out loud, it comes out all sing-songy. Everything sounds exactly the same. She wouldn't know an emotion if she tripped over one."

"Gee, Max. I guess you take this stuff pretty seriously," I smile at him.

"It's not that. But if you're gonna get up there in front of all those people, you don't want to look like a complete dork. So, you gotta at least try to do it right." Max squirms in his seat. I realize, suddenly, that he's really into this. In fact, he's not relaxed at all. He's just really good at acting like he doesn't care, like it's all the same to him. Of course, it all makes sense now. . . he's a natural born actor.

I watch as Mr. Kirby's victims go up on stage, two by two. Maybe I should be listening, to size up the competition, but I can't focus. I don't know what to do. It's like I need permission from someone—or something—to do this thing. And I can't figure out if I've got it. Or how to get it. I just don't know. And not knowing, suddenly, is unbearable. I lunge out of my chair and head for the door.

"Fran? What's going on?" Max twists around in his seat, calling after me. "Aren't you going to audition?"

"You were right. I think I am gonna hurl. I'll be fine. Good luck." And with that, I'm out of there.

Chapter 7

I peer out through the blue lace curtains above my window seat. There are veins of frost on the window. I blow out warm breath to try and clear it. Nothing out there but brown grass, bare limbs, a steel-gray sky, and a dusting of frost. What else did I expect? A Thanksgiving parade marching down my street? A flock of turkeys gobbling on the lawn, begging for their lives? It's still too early for company, thank God. I should still be sleeping; it's only eight. What a waste. But my whole body is buzzing. Bill Kirby's loud voice keeps booming in my head, issuing imaginary stage directions.

Now enter stage right! . . . You're distraught. . . . not angry, not in pain, I said distraught. . . I'm not feeling it, Singer. Show me!

I shake my head—actually shake it—to get Mr. Kirby out of there. Stupid. Don't think about it. I log onto my computer for distraction. Too early to IM anybody; nobody but me would be up at this hour, on a holiday. So I surf the Web instead. Play a few rounds of electronic solitaire. Playing cards on the computer is sort of like meditating—it puts a big chunk of your brain to sleep, which is a relief. *Move the ten of hearts onto the jack of hearts. . . now place the three of spades onto the four of spades. . . .breathe deeply and exhale slowly. . . .*

"Fran? You up?" Toby pokes his head around my door, which is only half-closed anyway. "I thought I heard you log on. Are you decent?"

"Where'd you get a phrase like that, 'Are you decent?' " I chuckle. "Do you even know what it means?" Toby sits down at my computer and starts surfing. "Hey, get off, Mister. Go bang your own keyboard."

48

"Yeah, I know what it means. I'm not a little brat, anymore, you know." I look at him and smile: he's wearing flannel pajamas with guitars and saxophones all over them, even though he doesn't play an instrument. Not a little kid? I should be so little again—and so free. I don't think Toby ever worries about anything—or ever even thinks beyond the next minute, or the next meal.

"Quick, close your eyes. Don't look down. Tell me what's on your pajamas."

"What's on them?" he asks, squinting his eyes shut and spinning around in my desk chair. "What do you mean, on them?"

"The pattern, idiot. What's the pattern on your pajamas?"

"I don't know, uh, little things, horns, or something."

"Hmm, close," I say, spinning him around rapidly on my swivel chair. He immediately tucks his legs and arms in, for a faster spin.

"I don't know, what," he says, clearly bored by the whole thing.

"Musical instruments." I stop the chair quickly—and his butt, encased in soft, slippery flannel, slides off and onto the floor.

"Hey!"

"Now vanish. Back to your own cave," I command.

"OK, but I came to ask you somethin'."

"What?"

"Is Mom, do you think, I mean, is she sick? Is there something going on that nobody's telling me? Cuz nobody ever tells me anything around here." Toby plucks at my keyboard again.

"No. I don't know. I mean, Mom's fine, I think. I don't think she likes selling houses."

"Oh, is that all? Is that why she's, I don't know, kind of tired and mopey? I mean, I was telling her yesterday after school all about these castles we're gonna be building, for the Middle Ages, and I was telling her about all the stuff I wanna buy to build my castle, and usually, she's all, like, tuned in and asking questions. But yesterday she was just kind of, 'Mmm, that's nice,

Toby,' like she wasn't even listening. And I gotta buy the stuff soon, you know, like next week."

"Yeah, I know she's been kind of distracted lately, that's true," I say, plucking Toby's grubby fingers off my keyboard. His nails are black with dirt. I guess Mom really hasn't been paying attention lately. "Why don't you ask Dad? He'll take you to the art supply store. He's good at that stuff, you know that."

"OK, I guess so."

"Now will you get out of here?"

"Yeah," he says, lingering in the doorway, his wrists shooting out of the cuffs of his flannel pajamas. "So, uh, you're OK, right? I mean you're not freaking out or anything, cuz one at a time is enough, y'know? I mean, is school OK and everything? I guess you made some new friends, huh?"

Maybe I was wrong about my baby brother. Maybe he isn't as totally clueless as I thought. "Sure," I say. "Everything's great. No worries. Too much homework, but you know. Now beat it."

Toby leaves, at last, and I throw open my closet, trying to decide what to wear today, to impress and amaze my relatives. But the thought of them all fawning, asking endless pointless questions. . . . And the questions behind my back, the hurried whispers with Mom or Dad in the kitchen, as if I didn't know.

I really don't need this.

I really can't take this.

I need to be left alone. To be let alone.

Everything isn't great, really. I mean, things are better. A whole lot better. But Fran 1.0 still needs an upgrade. Or an overhaul. And that's way more work than the makeover Cynthia, Leo, and Katie tried to give me.

I slide my quilt off the bed, wrap myself up in it as tightly as a cocoon, and lie on the floor, my head on my meditation pillow.

What would Peter say if he saw me right now? I don't know. I don't want to know. And I don't care.

But damn, there he is, front and center. Right smack between my closed eyes.

"Eat the blame."

Half the time—no, almost all the time—I have no idea what he's talking about. But he keeps on talking, anyway.

Don't run from your pain or your feelings, he says. Nothing is as horrible as it seems when we accept it, as when we are trying to run from it.

Yeah? And your point is?

You don't fool me. You know what my point is. You tell me.

You're telling me not to put up a wall between then and now. You're telling me to return to Hell and stay there.

No, Fran, that's not what I'm saying and you know it. I'm spending all this time with you to help you, not hurt you.

You're torturing me. I need to forget. Help me to forget—not to remember.

I can't do that, and it's not good for you. All of your experiences are part of you—who you are. You can't cut them out. That's like cutting off your arm or your leg. You have to accept those experiences—all of them.

I can see Peter, big bulky Peter, as if he were right here in the room with me. Clear as day. He's wearing his thick, frameless glasses—so clear you can see right through to his over-magnified blue eyes. Eyes that seem to look straight into you, asking questions you cannot, will not, answer.

Learning to live is learning to let go.

No, no, no, no.

I'm trying.

Part II

Winter 2005

Chapter 8

Fran Singer stands on top of a mountain. Well, not a mountain, but a slope. A big one, covered in white powdery snow. She grips her ski poles, lowers herself into a springy-kneed crouch. . . and *one, two, three*. . . the cold clear air stings her cheeks and the tips of her ears as she *shushes* down the trail, digging in her edges like an expert. She can hear an announcer in her head, calling the race.

And it's Singer, number 23, in first place...her time at the split gives her a solid lead over her competitors. Just look at her race down that mountain, ladies and gentlemen. Singer is hot, today. And it looks like there's a gold medal waiting for her at the base of the slope. . . .

Fran wishes her dad could see her right now, mastering this hill. She digs in her edges, as fiercely as though she were digging in at him. Fran had walked out of the ski hut earlier that day, her eyes blinded by tears of rage and frustration. As the family was renting skis, her father, Charlie Singer, had suggested—had been stupid enough to suggest—that Fran might not want to tackle the red D trail on the far side, as it was one of the most advanced and dangerous hills, and this was their first trip of the season. Perhaps she should get in a little practice first. Fran exploded, right in front of all the other families waiting in line to rent skis. Thank God Tracy wasn't there to witness her loss of control; she was off getting an early start on a lesson with a ski instructor.

"What! What are you saying, Dad? Did you ask Toby to do that, 'cuz I didn't hear you!" Fran had shouted, red-faced.

"Honey, calm down. Dad was only saying—" interjected her mother, Carla Singer, in a futile effort to bring Fran down a notch. "People are staring."

"I don't care! Thanks a lot for the insult, Dad! I guess I'm really still a baby, huh? Maybe I'm really Toby's *younger* sister, huh? Maybe I just won't ski at all now!" Fran knew she was losing it—but for her father to suggest that she, who has been skating every winter since she was a toddler—may not be as good as she thinks. Or worse, that Toby, the little squirt, might be better, is beyond infuriating. It's unfair. It's insensitive. So on the slope—the D slope, after all—Fran grits her teeth and crouches low, urging her skis on faster.

"'Scuse me! Comin' through! Watch out!" At that moment—just before Fran can clinch the imaginary gold medal and prove her father's lack of faith in her to be a big, big mistake—Toby comes racing past here, flinging icy snow behind him. Well, he's fast, but his form is terrible, Fran thinks. He's not better than I am, she thinks, he's sloppier. The judges would deduct points from his score, for sure.

"See ya later, alligator!" Toby yells, as he sails past her recklessly—careening down the slope, as only a heedless nine-year-old lacking any sense of fear or danger whatsoever would do. Fran catches up to him a few minutes later, as Toby stands at the base of the slope, catching his breath, his cheeks bright red and chapped.

"Hey, I'm going in for some hot chocolate? Wanna come?" Toby asks his sister, dragging a sleeve across his very runny nose.

"Nah, I'm gonna go find Tracy." Fran is still feeling out of sorts, and knows that if she hooks up with Tracy, her mood will change.

"Oh, right, she's on the *bunny* slope," says Toby, dismissively. "What a wimp." Fran ignores him, and sidesteps her way across the base of the mountain to the beginner slope, where her best friend Tracy is having her first skiing lesson. The Singers have been coming up to ski in Vermont over winter break for as long as Fran can remember. Her dad's parents own a cabin—a real log cabin—close to the Dartmouth Skiway, so every December, usually between Hanukkah and Christmas, the family piles into the old Subaru and drives up from Maryland. Each year, by Thanksgiving, Fran is so excited about the trip, she secretly starts crossing off days on a calendar she keeps in her bedroom.

55

This year, for the first time, the Singers let Fran invite Tracy. After all, the girls were both about to turn 13—old enough to look after themselves, for the most part. And besides, pairing the girls off meant there'd be less friction between Fran and Toby. Actually, Carla and Charlie would have been happy to bring Tracy along several years running—they knew her almost as well as their own daughter—but they never pressed when Tracy's mother said no. They figured she had her reasons; perhaps she just liked keeping the family close at holiday time.

Fran yells encouragement, as Tracy snowplows unsteadily down the hill.

"Good job! That's it! Don't be afraid, you can do it!" At last, Tracy makes her way to the bottom. Fran laughs. "You look about six in that ski suit. All puffed up."

"Aw, c'mon. Do I really look that ridiculous?" Tracy asks, despairing. "I feel like I'm six again," she says, digging her ski poles into the packed snow.

"No," Fran says, still laughing, "but remember that time when we were marshmallows for Halloween?"

"Yeah, I remember. We wrapped ourselves in white sheets and then stuffed them with toilet paper."

"So we started out all puffy and fat—"

"—and ended up looking more like skinny ghosts at the end—"

"—trailing streams of toilet paper behind us!" The two recall the same mental picture: Fran with her long brown hair, always braided, and Tracy with lighter, wispier dirty-blonde hair, big brown eyes, and a small dimple in her chin, whenever she laughs.

"So you're saying I look like a marshmallow? Gee that's encouraging. Listen, Miss Fancy Pants, how'd you get so good at this skiing stuff, anyway? It's really hard."

"We've been doing it forever, you know that. Maybe you just have to start when you're little. I'm not so good, anyway—just ask my dad. And I wish you'd been coming with us all these years. I would've had a lot more fun, and you'd've learned to ski."

"Yeah, well," says Tracy vaguely. "You know my mother. If there's fun to be had, you can be sure, she'll see to it that I don't have it." Tracy squints away into the sun.

"Oh, she's not that bad," says Fran. "You always bad-mouth her. She's just a little, well, over-protective, maybe."

"That's one way to put it. Look, I'm wiped. Can we go in and have hot chocolate?" Tracy asks, releasing her ski boots before Fran has a chance to reply.

"So you're done skiing? Wanna go down just one more time?" Fran asks, hoping her friend—usually so adventurous—changes her mind.

"No, no more. The guy who gave me the lesson was really obnoxious."

"I thought he seemed nice—at least in the beginning."

"Yeah, he was nice, but he treated me like such a baby. I just want to feel normal again—and I don't feel normal on skis!" The girls clomp into the ski hut—a big wooden building that sold snacks, hot drinks, and all sorts of fancy ski equipment and clothing. Carla Singer, is already seated at a wooden table, her heavily socked feet propped up on a bench, a steaming cup of coffee in her hands. Carla loves to ski, but after three hours on the slopes, she's reached her limit.

"So," asks Carla, "how'd it go, Tracy?"

"Good, I guess," Tracy says. "But I'm not sure skiing is my sport. I think I'll stick to field hockey and lacrosse." Carla laughs.

"It does take some getting used to," she says. "I remember when I met Fran's dad, I'd never been skiing before. I knew he really liked me when he spent hours going up and down the bunny slope with me, until I got the hang of it."

"Oooh, Dad was your ski instructor? I never knew that," Fran says, still mad at him—but impressed by the vision of her young future parents riding up the lift, gazing into each other's eyes. "That's so romantic."

"Well, not exactly—"

Where is Dad, anyway?" Fran asks, unzipping her ski jacket.

"Guess," says Carla.

"Racing down one of the back diamond trails with Toby?"

"Yup," Carla replies.

"Mom," Fran says, "does Dad realize that Toby has absolutely no common sense—that he'd ski down a lamp post? He could get hurt!"

Carla laughs again. "Honey, have you seen how many kids go whizzing down that slope? He'll be all right. I think the worst that could happen is he lands hard on his bottom. Besides, Dad's keeping an eye on him."

"I don't know, Mom. Once Dad starts hotdogging out there, he sort of forgets everything else. C'mon, Trace, let's get our own table." The girls march off in their socks to get snacks. Fran couldn't help thinking that sometimes, her mother seemed just a little too carefree. Didn't she worry, even for an instant, about her brainless young son skiing down that mountain at breakneck speed? I like to go fast too, Fran thought, but I'm not crazy. Well, she thinks, if Mom's not worried, I guess I shouldn't be, either. Besides, if Toby broke a leg or something, it wouldn't be my fault. He'd be asking for it.

Moments after the girls sit down, there seems to be some sort of commotion just outside the ski hut. Two big guys on skis, wearing green zippered jackets with the Dartmouth logo and dark sunglasses, rush by, talking loudly into walkie-talkies.

"Yes, the Northwest slope. About two-thirds of the way down. Next to that stand of tall firs. . . . Good. . . we'll meet you there." Without saying a word, Fran and Tracy carry their brownies and their hot cocoa over to the picture window, for a better look at what's going on. As the two Dartmouth guys headed up the ski lift, an ambulance pulls into the parking lot, and two more men get out carrying a white stretcher—exactly like the kind you see in movies, Fran thinks. Somebody crashed, obviously. Probably somebody who wasn't good enough to hurl down one of the steeper trails. I hope whoever it is didn't slam into a tree, she thinks.

"This can't be good," says Tracy, with a thrill in her voice.

"It happens all the time, though," says Fran. "Let's go out and watch." The girls quickly find their snow boots and headed for the door. "Mom, wanna come?" Carla Singer waves them on.

"Go ahead and report back to me. I want to sit and finish my coffee."

The girls squint in the bright sunlight, made even brighter by the whitely glinting snow. Looking up the mountain, they see a clump of people who look like they're all hunched over, more or less in a circle. The men from the ambulance had taken the stretcher up in the ski lift, and now two ski instructors are carrying it carefully down the slope, toward the crowd.

"Do you think it's serious?" Tracy asks.

"Probably not," Fran replies. "Somebody gets hurt practically every time we come here. But it's usually no big deal. Maybe a broken ankle, or something, but nothing life-threatening." As their feet slowly grow numb in the cold, Fran and Tracy watch as the stretcher-bearers carry someone—it looks like a big person, probably an adult—over to the ski-lift side of the mountain, where the ambulance has crept up an emergency access road to meet them. Suddenly, a lone figure breaks away from the crowd on the mountain and comes hurtling toward them on skis, swerving rapidly from side to side.

"It's Toby," Fran says. Toby reaches the bottom and slides over to them. "So, what's going on?"

"It's Dad, Fran!" Toby's face is bright red and he's gasping for breath. Fran feels her stomach lurch—suddenly she doesn't feel like a spectator anymore. This isn't just another accident. Tracy instinctively puts her arm around her friend's shoulder. And secretly, she's only too happy to do it. It seems that usually, it's Fran taking care of her, one way or another. Now the tables are reversed, for once. "We were doing great, and then he hit a bump

59

or a rock or something, and the next thing I knew, he wasn't skiing next to me," Toby gasps. "I stopped half-way down and turned back, and there he was in the snow, with his skis all twisted up."

"Oh, God," says Fran. "Toby, run into the hut and tell Mom. She's sitting at one of the tables. We'll head over to the ambulance and find out what's going on." Fran has a weird sensation: She hears herself issuing orders to Toby, and she can feel her legs moving under her. But she feels strangely disconnected from the whole thing, like she's having a dream in which she's was watching somebody else go through this experience. Dad was going to be OK, of course. Of course Dad was OK. Nothing really bad could happen to him because—well, because it just couldn't. And he was a really strong skier. He'd been skiing his whole life. A stupid rock couldn't really mess him up, could it? In a flash, Fran is desperately sorry she'd yelled at her dad that morning; he was just trying to protect her. But then another guilty thought creeps in: He's the one who's hurt, not she. Maybe he needed someone to protect *him*. . . and there was no one to do it. Her father looks after her, that's his job, Fran realizes, but who looks after him? Suddenly, she realizes that maybe he's just as vulnerable as everyone else.

Fran and Tracy grab hands and run toward the ambulance. Fran wants desperately to see her dad—but at the same time, a part of her doesn't want to see him at all. What if he looks different? What if he's bloody? What if he's crying? Fran doesn't think she could stand to see that—it would be like watching a stranger taking over her father's body. All these thoughts flash by in a split second—by which time, Fran sees her dad lying in the back of the ambulance. A woman with a stethoscope—someone the girls hadn't seen before, during the crisis—is gently prodding his leg.

"Dad! Dad!" Fran pushes her way past the ambulance driver and a policeman to reach the back of the ambulance. Tracy follows right behind her. "What happened? Are you OK? Are you bleeding? Is anything broken?" Without thinking, Fran begins climbing into the back of the ambulance, which is crammed with all sorts of supplies—metal boxes with red crosses on them, oxygen tanks, and all sorts of stuff Fran can't identify.

"Whoa, hold on there, honey!" says the woman hovering over Charlie Singer. "Three's a crowd back here."

"Dad?" Fran kneels inside the ambulance, squinting to adjust to the dark interior. The woman begins cutting off Charlie's Singer's pants leg with a big pair of shears. "Is it broken?"

"I'm afraid so," Charlie replies. "It sure as heck feels broken," he says, wincing as the woman—wearing a blue ski jacket with an EMT patch—continues working on his leg. Fran reaches for her father's hand. She hasn't held his hand in a long time, but it just feels like the right thing to do. She squeezes his hand, offering a silent apology. He squeezes back—she knows he accepts it.

"Your face, Dad," says Fran. "It's all scratched up. You look terrible. Like you were in a plane crash, or something."

"Oh, it's just scraped from the ice, pumpkin. Not serious. I'll be OK, really. Where's your mom?" He sounds OK, Fran thinks, but he's awfully pale. And those scrapes—all red and purple, with scratch marks down his cheeks.

"I told Toby to go get her."

"Here they come," says Tracy, feeling helpless and embarrassed. What's a family friend to do at a time like this? Tracy and Fran have been best friends since pre-school, so she's practically a sister—and the Singers are her second family. But how are you supposed to act at a time like this? I guess the best thing is just to stand back and stay out of everybody's way, Tracy thinks. But if Charlie were her dad, she'd be in there squeezing the life out of him—something she can't imagine doing with her own step-dad.

"Charlie? What's happened? Are you all right?" Carla rushes up to the ambulance, with Toby beside her. Now all the Singers try to crowd into the rear of the ambulance, but the EMT lady shoos them out.

"Folks, I can only take one of you in the ambulance with me to the hospital. We've got to take some x-rays and set these bones," she says in a no-nonsense tone of voice, a stethoscope swinging from her neck.

"How bad is the break, do you think?" Carla asks.

"We won't know for sure until we see the x-rays, but I'd say he's got a compound tib-fib fracture and probably also tore the heck out of his knee cartilage. My guess is he'll be on crutches for quite awhile. Might even need surgery. We'll have to see--"

"Cool!" says Toby, though he has no idea what a tib-fib fracture is. "Dad, can I ride with you in the ambulance?"

"Damn!" says Charlie.

"Whoa, Dad, you said—"

"I know what I said, Toby. Never mind," says Charlie, wincing. "That's what I get for trying to keep up with you!"

"I'll ride with Dad," says Carla. "Fran, I guess you and Tracy should stay right here—in the ski hut—with Toby until we sort this out. No more skiing today."

"Aww, but Mom—" says Toby.

"One of the officers can drive the kids to the hospital, ma'am," says the EMT lady, nodding toward the uniformed police officers milling near the ambulance.

"Thank you," says Carla, climbing into the ambulance, taking Charlie's hand, which is still warm from Fran's grasp. "Kids, get your stuff and we'll meet you at the hospital. When you get there, go to the information desk and ask them to find us. They'll know what to do. And listen to the police officer!" Like who wouldn't, Fran thinks. The EMT closes the ambulance doors, the red lights begin flashing and the siren starts blaring—causing Fran, Tracy, and Toby to practically jump out of their snow boots.

That's my Mom, thinks Fran. Real cool in an emergency. I hope I'm like that when I grow up. The take-charge type—the one who always knows the right thing to do in a tricky situation. And who doesn't blow up at the slightest set-back. But right now, Fran realizes, backing away from the ambulance, her legs feel like Jell-

62

O and she's still got adrenalin pumping through her body, making her feel short of breath. Not a very take-charge-like attitude, she thinks. Well, at least she can still take charge of Toby.

"C'mon Tobe. Let's get our stuff. Where'd you leave your skis? Hurry up." The three of them return to the ski hut to gather their things.

"It's gonna be OK," says Tracy. "Your dad was pretty lucky, really."

"I know," says Fran. "I'm not worried." She takes a final look up the slope where her dad fell. The afternoon sun has begun its descent, casting an intense gray-blue glare across the white slope. Somehow, the mountain looks different now, Fran thinks, like a big beast keeping secrets deep inside its slippery, snowy bulk.

Later that night, the Singer family and Tracy all lie sprawled, like exhausted marathoners at the end of a long race, across soft rugs and a comfy sofa. A fire is blazing in the black cast iron stove that Charlie's parents installed when they built the cabin. A long black stove pipe carries smoke from the fireplace up into the chimney, and then out into the cold winter air. When the fire's going—which is practically all the time, when the cabin is occupied in winter—the house looks from a distance like an enchanted wooden cottage, with its cheery white puffs of smoke wandering out into the woods, as a greeting. At least, that's what Fran has always thought, as they come up the long gravel drive to the cabin, which is shrouded in dark woods. After hours of skiing, and Charlie Singer's ordeal, and more hours spent hanging around the hospital, everyone has returned to the cabin absolutely exhausted and famished. Several empty buckets of take-out fried chicken and empty mashed potato containers lie strewn across the wooden table in the kitchen. Carla and Charlie have polished off a bottle of wine. Charlie's right leg is in a cast that runs from his thigh to his ankle. The leg is propped up across a footstool, and a pair of crutches rests nearby. The cast already is covered with colored magic marker lines—hearts, silly faces, a crude drawing of a person falling off of skis, and of course the kids' autographs. Toby is mindless pushing buttons on his Gameboy, and Fran and Tracy are playing a card game called Spit, which involves a lot of rapid slapping of cards. The card game is a fallback position: both Fran and Tracy would much rather have been on a cell phone, recounting the day's drama to about six of their friends. There's nothing more fun than telling a story full of danger and excitement when you know there's a happy ending—or at least not a tragic one. But there's no cell service from the cabin, up here in the Vermont woods. So they had to content themselves with something a lot more old-fashioned.

"You know, Dad," says Fran, taking a break from card-slapping, "you look just like an overgrown Tiny Tim sitting there." By now, all the anger she had directed toward him so fiercely that morning has drained away, and she realizes how much she loves him, even when he's driving her crazy. But she'd never actually tell him that, of course.

"God bless us, every one!" says Charlie in a squeaky fake British accent, as everyone breaks into laughter.

"I'm still hungry!" says Toby, looking up from his Gameboy.

"Me, too!" says Fran. "Let's make s'mores!" Without further encouragement, Fran and Tracy rummage around in the kitchen for a bag of marshmallows, a box of graham crackers, and some bars of Hershey chocolate. They find all three in the pantry. Soon, all three kids have skewered pieces of kindling pulled from the box of logs next to the fireplace, and are putting s'mores together as fast as they can toast the marshmallows. Fran and Toby make extras for Carla and Charlie—who like to eat them, but don't want to cook them.

Fran looks around at her family, her best friend at her side, and feels the hard rush from the day, all that adrenalin, leaking out of her. Suddenly, Fran is so sleepy, she can hardly keep her eyes open. She looks over at Tracy, whose every expression is as familiar to Fran as those of her own family. Sure enough, Tracy's eyes have that glazed look. And she watches her dad stuffing a gooey s'more into his mouth, as her mother leans forward to catch the bits of graham cracker sliding down his shirt. Fran never would have imagined that the blaring ambulance pulling into the Dartmouth Skiway parking lot earlier in the day, and all the people gathered on the hill, could have had anything to do with her family. Nothing like this had ever happened to them before, Fran thinks. I guess we've always sort of lived in a bubble, and today the bubble burst. But anyway, she thinks, it's over and done, and nothing like this is ever likely to happen again. Freak accidents don't just pop up out of the blue every day, she concludes. Especially not to us—the boring, predictable Singer family.

Chapter 9

It's Monday morning and winter break is over. Fran's alarm goes off promptly at six-fifty, startling her awake with the sound of chirping birds. It's enough to fool you into thinking for a minute that it's spring, instead of a cold, dark winter morning in January. Fran reaches across her bed to slap the alarm button—and then abruptly remembers: I cannot see or hear, she tells herself. The alarm doesn't count. Now I can't see or hear. So. Fran gropes her way out of bed, and practically falls flat on her face tripping over a furry pink slipper (of course, she can't see that it's pink, but she knows what it is as soon as she steps on it, turning her ankle a bit). She walks cautiously out into the hallway toward the bathroom, her eyes closed and her arms extended out in front of her, like a sleepwalker.

"What the heck are you doing?" asks Toby loudly, heading to the bathroom himself. "You look like a complete idiot." Fran ignores him and continues walking slowly, crookedly, like a drunken sailor. "Mom, Fran is acting crazy! She's lost her marbles! Better come check it out!" Toby yells. Carla's already down in the kitchen, brewing coffee and setting out milk and cereal. Charlie takes a lot longer to get ready these days—the cast slows him down a lot.

"Kids? Come on, time to get ready!" Carla calls up stairs.

"But Mom—" says Toby.

"Toby, Fran's just practicing for the play," Carla shouts back. She knows without looking exactly what Fran is up to. It's just one of those mom things. "Ignore her and get dressed."

"Geez! Why doesn't anybody tell me these things! Get going there, blindy, I gotta use the bathroom!" Toby tells his sister.

Rehearsals for *The Miracle Worker* begin in earnest this afternoon, at three-fifteen sharp. Practically everybody knows the story of Helen Keller, the girl born more than a century ago, who became famous because even though she was blind and deaf, she still managed to write all sorts of books and give speeches all over the country about overcoming handicaps. Helen Keller was born with all her senses functioning normally, but she got very sick when she was little, and even though she eventually got better, by then she had lost her sight and her hearing. Her teacher, Annie Sullivan, who lived with the Kellers in their big Alabama home for much of Helen's childhood, taught her to read and write using Braille. She even taught her how to use a knife and fork at the table—since she couldn't see them, how could she know what they were for? Fran knows the story backwards and forwards. She's read two biographies of Helen Keller and of course she's read the play a thousand times. To Fran, the real miracle isn't Helen Keller's story—it's the fact that Fran got the lead part. She's Helen Keller. The star. Well, to be fair, the Annie Sullivan character is a star, too. And guess who gets to play her? Tracy Guilford! What could be better?

Fran will never forget the day the girls learned they'd gotten the parts. The tryouts had been terrifying: Everybody who wanted a part had to come up on stage, in the school auditorium, and read from the play—a play they'd never seen before, much less heard of—with the seventh grade drama teacher, Harriet Birnbaum. Ms. Birnbaum has a sharp pointy nose and chin—like the Wicked Witch of the West, Fran can't help thinking—and a high, sharp voice. She was always talking and moving very fast, like she'd had too much caffeine, Fran thought. But it wasn't her rapid, birdlike movements that struck fear and terror into students' hearts. It was the fact that she didn't seem to realize that people had feelings—that they could, in fact, be embarrassed, shamed, or humiliated. Take Mike, for example. Fran and Tracy watched from their seats in the auditorium as little Mikey—he hasn't hit his growth spurt yet, and Fran and Tracy feel sort of protective towards him, since they'd all been together since kindergarten—reads the part for Captain Keller, Helen's father. Captain Keller is supposed to be stern and bossy, the guy who's always in charge. So Mikey's up there reading the part, and Harriet Birnbaum is playing Mrs. Keller, a gentle southern belle who's meek and mild. Well, Ms. Birnbaum must be a pretty good actress, Fran thinks, if she can look and act like the meek and mild sort, since she's really a dragon lady. Anyway, Mike's just reading the script for the first time—you gotta cut him some slack, since he hasn't had a chance to look it over first or even think about it. And Ms. Birnbaum just rips into him.

"Mr. Shuster!" she says, slapping her script against her thigh. "You are not some shrimpy little seventh grader here! You're the man of the house! The boss! The big enchilada! What you say, goes! So don't be such a wimp, Shuster!"

Well, after that little speech, Mike stood for a minute, his face all red, his hair sort of plastered to his forehead.

"Oh my God," Tracy whispers to me. "That was so unbelievably mean. I can't believe she said that to him. God, Fran, I don't know about this—"

"Well, wait," Fran whispers back. "Let's see what happens."

Nothing much does happen. Mike stumbles through the part and Ms. Birnbaum mumbles a thank you when he's done. "Next!" she yells.

Tracy goes first, simply because she's sitting one seat closer to the end of the row than Fran. Fran watches as Tracy walks onstage; she can feel her own heart beating fast—probably as fast as Tracy's. Fran refuses to think about the fact that she and her best friend are actually sort of competing against each other. The way they worked it out was, they'll each just try out, and if one gets a part and the other doesn't, each girl swears she'll support her friend.

"Look, it's just a stupid play," Tracy had said. "I don't think it should affect our friendship."

"Yeah, I hope I'm not that superficial," Fran had replied. "Really, I hope you get a good part," she had said—and meant it. But still, Fran knew that deep, deep down, she desperately wanted to be Helen Keller. It wasn't anything against Tracy. It was just that she thought she could do a really convincing job. She didn't know much about Helen Keller at that point, but she had this feeling deep in her gut that it was something she wanted to do— and something she could do. Up to now, Fran hadn't really been good at anything. She played the flute—but not very well. And she didn't practice like she should have. Toby was already the star of his fourth grade soccer league—not that that meant anything, but it was obvious he was really good at it, and he cared about it. But Fran had always felt like a big blank, a big zero. Ready for something—ready to be someone—but who? And how? And when? She told herself that this theatre stuff might be her thing—if she could just get over her fear of Birnbaum, her fear of standing up on that stage in the glaring white light, with everybody staring at her, and her fear of all those pages and pages of script she'd have to memorize if she did manage to get cast. Other than that— no big deal, right?

Ms. Birnbaum asks Tracy to read a few pages of Helen Keller, then a few pages of Annie Sullivan, and then some more of Mrs. Keller. Fran watches intently, wanting Tracy to do a really good job—but maybe not a better job than Fran thinks she can do herself. It's a little more complicated than I thought, Fran thinks. And she has to admit, Tracy is good. Even her brown wavy hair has an old-fashioned sort of look—or it could, with a few minor adjustments—that you'd expect somebody in a play like this to have. And her southern accent! Fran had never heard Tracy put on a southern accent, since she's spent her whole life in Maryland (which used to be considered the South, but really wasn't anymore). But there it was. "Mrs. Keller" was just so full of *south'n chahm* and *oh, suh, ah do declare!*, Fran could hardly believe it was the same person. Fran couldn't help feeling just a teeny tiny bit jealous: Maybe Tracy was better at this than she was.

Maybe she, Fran, would never be that good at anything—and never better than anyone else. So when Ms. Birnbaum finally said to Tracy, "Dial it back a bit dear. This isn't *Gone With the Wind*. You're laying it on a bit too thick. In fact, I'm not quite sure the audience would even understand you if you pile on that much dialect," Fran felt two things at once: indignation, on Tracy's behalf, and relief, on her own.

When Tracy retook her seat next to Fran, she was trembling all over, and breathing in short, shallow gasps. Fran put a hand on her shoulder. "You were awesome, Trace. I know she's gonna cast you." Tracy could only manage a weak smile, at that point.

And then it was Fran's turn. As she headed onstage, she feared for a second she was going to pass out, her heart was beating so fast, and everything looked a bit dim. She knew now what people meant when they said their hearts were in their mouths. She could feel a big lump expanding through her chest into her throat, almost choking off her air supply. But when Ms. Birnbaum put the script in her hands, something unusual happened—at least, it had never happened to Fran before. The words seemed to leap off the page and enter straight into her brain—not even her brain, really, but her emotional core. She could just feel what the words on the page meant to convey. She could feel the personality of the part, like she'd been injected with it. There was no time to analyze this process, or to figure how or why it was happening, but it was. Fran read Helen Keller and Annie Sullivan scenes. And as she did, she felt herself become each person; the script seemed to speak right through her. She never did get to read Mrs. Keller—which was a good thing, since she didn't think she could do such a good Southern accent.

When her audition was over, Ms. Birnbaum said little. She made a few quick notes on a pad, which she'd done for everybody immediately after their audition. "OK, you can go," was all Fran got. "Who's next?"

A week later, the list went up on a bulletin board in the middle school hallway. Fran and Tracy had agreed to go look at it together—and told each other they wouldn't freak out, no matter what. A small crowd had gathered, but the type was too small to read from a distance, so Fran and Tracy had to wait before shouldering their way in. Fran saw Mike Shuster scan the list quickly, then just as quickly turn away, looking like he hadn't a care in the world.

"Mikey?" Fran said, knowing the outcome already.

"It's OK. I didn't really want to do it, anyway," Mike said. "I'd rather play basketball." Mikey was probably too small for basketball, Fran thought, but what the heck. Mike shrugged and walked away, his backpack slung across one shoulder. Tracy gave Fran a little shove.

"Go look," she said.

"No, you go."

"I thought we were doing this together?" Tracy said, and both girls walked up to the bulletin board. At first, Fran couldn't take her eyes off her own name...and the name that was linked to it: Helen Keller. *Fran Singer. . . Helen Keller.* She let her eyes travel across the little dots on the page, connecting the two names. She was Helen Keller. No. Not possible. Fran's eyes didn't even make it the rest of the way down the list. She felt a little bit like she did when Toby told her on the ski slope that their dad had been injured. Funny how your body reacts to bad news and good news pretty much the same way. Basically, Fran was ready to puke. Suddenly, she felt someone pushing her, shaking her. It was Tracy, jumping up and down.

"I can't believe it! I can't believe it! This is just too cool! You and me!" Fran couldn't figure out what Tracy was talking about. She, Fran, was Helen Keller—what on earth did Tracy mean? She looked at the list once more, and this time she saw it: *Tracy Guilford. . .Annie Sullivan.*

"Oh. My. God," Fran said slowly. Tracy was still pushing Fran's shoulder, and pumping her arm. "This is almost too good to be true," Fran said, grinning widely.

And now, finally, the play rehearsals were actually beginning. And everything had worked out well—at least for Fran and Tracy. Fran was Helen, Tracy was Annie. Two equals in history, two equals as friends, doing the theater thing together. Fran was grateful they'd get to share all the in-jokes together—the ones that develop when you're spending hours and hours rehearsing a play that bears no resemblance to your actual life. Come to think of it, if one of them had gotten a part, and one hadn't, a new gap in their friendship might have opened, Fran thinks. The two had been sharing inside jokes since they were little girls. What would it be like if they couldn't continue? Fran was glad, and deeply relieved, that she and Tracy wouldn't have to pull away from each other over this.

The night, with the first rehearsal over, Fran slips into her Helen Keller routine again at home by trying to set the table for dinner with her eyes closed. This time, she's got a black sleep mask over her eyes that's hooked behind her ears, and she's stuffed a pair of latex earplugs into her ears. She got them from her dad, who uses them at noisy construction sites.

"Mmm, not too bad, Helen," her mother shouts from just a few feet away, by the stove. The kitchen smells delicious—roast chicken and rice. Fran is grateful that Helen Keller could at least smell. The earplugs don't really block out all the noise, so Fran can actually hear what her mother is saying—but she's pretending she can't. "If you don't mind the fact that your fork is about half a mile to the left of your plate, and your knife is north of it," Carla Singer says. "But, not bad. Keep at it, Helen, you'll improve." Suddenly, Fran feels her mother by her side. "I have to run out and get your dad downtown. He's been at the site all day and I'll bet he'll be awfully sore." Charlie Singer can't drive with his leg in an extended cast, so Carla has to drive him to and from work. Luckily, he's supervising a local job—a high-rise condominium complex going up near the harbor—so he hasn't had to miss work. "Earplugs or no earplugs, turn the rice off in ten minutes, when the timer goes off," Carla tells Fran. "And don't let your brother eat any potato chips when he comes in from soccer." Fran nods to show she's heard. She's trying to stay in character, but it isn't easy when you're being handed a bunch of instructions by your mother.

At dinner—which Fran has agreed to participate in using all her senses—her dad sits with his broken leg propped up on an extra chair. By now, there's hardly any white plaster showing, so thoroughly have Fran and Toby drawn on it—and Toby's friends, too, over the weekend.

"Ahhh!" Charlie Singer suddenly lets out a yelp, dropping his fork. Carla turns to him anxiously.

"What is it? Are you in pain? I knew you shouldn't have been on your feet all day down there, even with those crutches. Maybe you do need to take a few weeks off—"

"No, it isn't that," Charlie says. "I've got an itch, a terrible itch, just above my knee. Imagine the worst, the meanest mosquito bite you've ever gotten—it's like that."

"I know what will help," says Carla. She fetches a shish kebab skewer from a kitchen drawer. "Here, reach down through the gap and scratch." Charlie carefully extends the long, thin metal stick down his leg, and breathes a sigh of relief.

"Fran, before I forget," says Carla, resuming her dinner. "Tonya called. She wants to know if you'd like to babysit for Theo Saturday night."

"You mean real babysitting? A night job?" Fran asks. She's been a mother's helper for Tonya Vining and her husband, Frank, and other neighbors, for almost two years, since she was eleven. But this would be her first real teenage babysitting job.

"Yes. Tonya said you could do it with a friend, since it's your first time. She thought it would be easier if there were two of you. Theo can be a real handful, I know," Carla says. Theo was a holy-terror three-year-old—tons of energy, a body built like a square tank, and no common sense, whatsoever. Sort of the way Toby was at that age—only worse, Fran decides. Toby actually ran out of steam, sometimes, and you could get him to sit and scribble

73

with crayons in a coloring book. Theo is like the Energizer Bunny—he just keeps going and going. But Fran knew she could handle him. She'd done it many times before, at the Vinings' house on weekends. In fact, the piggy bank in her room—not actually a pig, but an oval ceramic box with a tiny lock and key—was stuffed with ones and fives. And there was more in the bank. Fran much preferred saving to spending—since once it was gone, it was gone.

"OK, great," Fran says. "Can I invite Tracy?"

"I don't see why not," Carla says. "She knows the Vinings, right?"

"Yeah. She's been over there a ton, too," Fran replies. "Hey, did she say how much she's gonna pay us?"

"My little entrepreneur," says Charlie. "Make sure you drive a hard bargain. Don't sell yourself cheap."

"Oh, Charlie," says Carla. Then, to Fran, "Why don't you call Tonya back yourself, and find out when she wants you over there, and be sure to let her know Tracy will come, too. You can work out the other details later."

"Hey, I wanna earn some money, too," says Toby, a greasy ring around his lips, from sucking on a drumstick.

"You, my friend," says his father, "can salt the driveway and the walkway—and find out if Mrs. Smith needs you to do hers, too. It's supposed get very icy, the next couple of days."

"OK," says Toby, happily. "That's worth at least ten dollars, right, Dad?"

"We'll see," says Charlie.

"Wait a minute," says Fran. "He can't earn more than I do. I've got more responsibility. Caring for somebody's kid is a lot more important than sprinkling salt on a driveway."

"Hold on," says Charlie, scratching his leg with a grimace. "We don't know who's going to earn what, yet. So far, I'm the only one making any real money around here, anyway."

"Well, if I could sell a house and get a commission—" adds Carla, shrugging.

74

"If only," adds Charlie. Fran can see that this issue about her mom making extra money is a thing between her parents—but she also sees that both her parents are quietly laughing about it. Maybe it's just not that important. As far as Fran can tell, nobody in this house is starving, at least.

It's back to homework and Helen Keller practice. Being deaf and blind is very hard work, Fran finds. It takes a lot of practice. But first things first; it's time to log on.

franonstage: i'm babysitting 4 theo sat nite. mrs vining said we could do it 2gether. want 2?
tracysouttahere: yes! nite! u kidding? we'll plan yr bday party.
franonstage: cool. after theo goes zzzz.
tracysouttahere: rite. gtg. ttyl.
franonstage: bye.

Chapter 10

The Vinings lived at the end of the block on the same street as the Singers, and one block over from the Guilford's. All three families had moved into the neighborhood—a quiet section of north Baltimore, lined with old houses, old trees, and big back yards—within a few years of one another. Tonya and Fred Vining had been among the last in the neighborhood to start a family—and many of the older girls who lived nearby, including Fran and Tracy, competed for a chance to help Mrs. Vining manage Theo. He was adorable, the girls agreed, with wispy blonde hair, a big round head, and a short, fat body with arms and legs that were far stronger than they appeared. Fran knew this from experience: she'd lifted and carried Theo since he was an infant, getting him in and out of his playpen or his crib. His little legs routinely pummeled her in the stomach—a preview of the super-energetic toddler he would become. Tonya Vining was quite relaxed, especially for a first-time mother. She was content to let the girls handle Theo for hours on end—or between feedings, anyway—while she caught up on housework, or just sat with a magazine and a cup of coffee. Tonya was one of a handful of stay-at-home mothers in the neighborhood, and everyone could see at a glance that managing Theo was a full-time job. Fred Vining helped out as much as he could—he didn't think twice about changing diapers, for instance—but he also traveled a lot on business. So Tonya needed all the local help she could get.

The Singers and the Vinings had been friends for years, since before Toby was born. The four adults used to spend long summer evenings together, sitting around on one back deck or another, drinking wine, discussing local real estate, politics, work, practically anything, really, while Fran slept soundly in her crib. So when Tonya called Carla to ask for Fran's help, it seemed the most natural thing in the world—and a clear sign, to both Carla and Fran, that Fran was indeed growing up.

The Vinings' house was practically a mirror image of Fran's, with an L-shaped kitchen, a small living room and dining room, and four bedrooms circled around the upstairs hallway. But there were two things the Vinings had done that distinguished their house from the others on the block. First, they turned the attic into a fancy master bedroom suite with a bathroom that had a Jacuzzi in it. Fran had been up there only once, to retrieve a toy of Theo's. She thought it looked like something you'd see in a magazine about fancy homes. The other thing the Vinings had done was to put a big in-ground pool in their backyard, with a large wooden deck alongside it. They were the only ones in the neighborhood with a pool, and it practically took up the entire yard. Tonya swam laps all summer; it was how she kept her gorgeous figure.

Fran and Tracy knew their way around this house about as well as their own. They knew which pantry cupboards Tonya kept the cookies in, and they knew precisely which freezer rack held containers of ice cream, when they were lucky enough to find some. Tonya had always told the girls to help themselves to anything they wanted, and to give Theo a Ritz cracker or two, at the same time. Theo couldn't stand to watch anybody else eat something, if he couldn't eat, too.

Carla and Charlie debated briefly, in private, whether to let Fran walk alone down the long quiet block to the Vinings on a cold and dark Saturday night. In the end, they decided there could be no real harm; as no one was likely to be out on a frigid January night, and Fran knew everyone in each of the houses she would pass. There seemed no point in making a big deal of it, so at seven o'clock on Saturday, Fran slips on her parka and heads over to the Vinings, where Tracy would meet her.

The moment Fran steps across the Vinings' threshold, Theo comes barreling towards her and wraps his arms around her legs. "Up! Up!" he instructs her. But the hefty three-year-old is almost too much for Fran to lift, so she kneels down to him instead.

"Fwan, come pway!" Theo instructs. He reminds her briefly of Toby, in his footie blue flannel pajamas lined with snaps. His soft blonde hair is wet and combed from a recent bath. He smells like baby: warm, and faintly scented with soap.

"Tracy's coming, Theo, Tracy's coming!" Fran tells him, adopting the loud, enthusiastic voice people so often use with babies. "Let's wait for Tracy!'

"I get my ball," Theo says, running off to the den as fast as his little covered feet will take him. Tonya Vining comes down the stairs and into the hallway, with Fred right behind her. She's all decked out, in a slinky cocktail dress, patterned stockings, sexy heels, and a dripping necklace. The front door opens and Tracy steps in, sweeping the cold air in with her.

"Perfect timing," says Tonya. "Girls, thank you so much. We couldn't do this without you." Both Fran and Tracy are dying to know what kind of fancy party the Vinings are going too—but they don't want to seem too nosy. Neither girl can imagine her parents getting this dressed up—Fred's wearing a crisp tuxedo—for anything. "Now, you know Theo. He's going to want to stay up and play with you. He won't want you to put him in his bed. Oh, did I tell you? We moved him out of the crib last week, because he started climbing out by himself, the little devil." Fran could easily picture it: a grunting little Theo pushing himself up and over the crib rail. "His bed has a guard rail, so don't worry about him falling out. But getting him into it will be another story. So do the best you can."

As Tonya continues issuing instructions, she bustles around, putting things into her beaded black evening bag, and checks her lipstick in the hallway mirror. Fran and Tracy try not to stare—but they want to take in every details of her ensemble. Fran nudges Tracy and whispers, "Do you think that necklace is real? Real diamonds, I mean?"

"Could be," Tracy whispers back. "I think they're loaded."

"Who says?" Fran whispers again.

"My mom thinks so," replies Tracy.

"Then why don't they live in a bigger house?" Fran asks, knowing this isn't the time to discuss the matter. Fran and Tracy had long agreed that Tonya Vining was the "hot" mom on the block—the one who looks more like a model than a mother. Fred walks around, turning out lights, and making sure the back door is locked. Despite the tuxedo, Fred Vining isn't handsome, Fran and Tracy agree. He's going bald on top, and his nose seems too large for his face. Privately, Fran thinks he isn't nearly as handsome as her own dad, and she wonders how he managed to convince such a beautiful woman to marry him.

"Well, girls," says Tonya. She's stunning in a long mink coat (Fran does wonder briefly whether any little animals suffered for that coat—but it's so elegant, she has to admit). Her makeup is just perfect, and her lips are a deep, shimmering red, just like the women in the TV commercials. "Help yourselves, of course, to anything in the kitchen. There's a tin of brownies on the counter." Fran cannot picture this glamorous woman baking brownies—but she has seen Tonya in her more ordinary moments, dressed in jeans and a sweater. Always elegant—but also a little closer to ordinary.

"We'll be home around midnight," says Fred Vining, in his deep, authoritative bass. "I assume Theo will be out by then—even he can't hold out forever. So if you girls get very sleepy, you can curl up on the couches in the living room." Fran and Tracy thank the Vinings, and wish them a good time. Neither girl thinks for an instant that she's going to fall asleep—there's too much to do.

By nine o'clock, the brownie tin holds nothing but crumbs. Fran and Tracy had agreed that they wouldn't let Theo have any— the chocolate and sugar might be too much for him before bedtime. So the girls took turns sneaking into the kitchen, claiming to each other they "needed to keep their strength up" in order to manage Theo. You wouldn't think one little boy could require so much management, but he almost seems capable of being in two places at once. One minute, he's building a giant tower with big, brightly colored wooden blocks, and the next, he's knocking them down, throwing them everywhere, and climbing up the back of the couch to reach for a round glass ornament that sits on a bookshelf. It's a paperweight, and it's got swirls of bright red and yellow inside it. Who wouldn't want to hold that? Anyway, you'd never think, for an instant, that something that breakable was in his reach—but once Theo set his sights on something, he clambers after it as if nothing were in his way.

"Theo! Get down from there!" Tracy had yelled gently, stuffing a brownie in her mouth. Theo turned from his perch—his knees balanced precariously on the back of the couch, his little hands grasping the bookshelf for balance.

"Cookie!" he yelled, perhaps smelling the brownie. You couldn't get much past Theo.

"No cookie, now, Theo. Story time," Fran told him.

"Choo-choo!" Theo replied, grasping a wooden boxcar in each hand, from a train set that lay scattered about. Fran and Tracy played choo-choo for what seemed like an hour, but in reality was barely 15 minutes. Theo would hook several wooden cars together, then run them along the carpet making choo-choo and whoo-whoo noises, in imitation of a train whistle. Fran and Tracy followed on their knees, making the same sounds he did. Pretty soon, the three of them were making a racket, whoo-whooing around the living room, the wooden train set in tow, a little plastic conductor seated up in the first car, wearing an engineer's gray-striped hat. Because the caboose kept tipping over, Theo stopped every few seconds to straighten out the whole thing and continue the journey.

At nine forty-five, Theo at last lies curled up on his bed, still as a sack of potatoes, breathing softly through his lips. A nightlight shaped like a rocket ship throws out a soft, yellowish glow into the room. Fran and Tracy had taken turns reading *Goodnight, Moon* at least six times, followed by at least four rounds of *If You Give a Mouse a Cookie*. Theo giggled and pointed at the pictures through every rendition, as though he'd never heard the books before, and had just discovered how delightful they were. Until, all of a sudden, he said "Night, night," and flopped over on his bed—asleep as soon as his little blonde wisps hit the pillow. Theo is just one big on-off switch, Fran thought.

The girls tiptoe out to the living room. They turn on the large flat-panel TV and flip channels for awhile, more for the thrill of staring at such a large screen, than because there's anything interesting on.

"We should practice our script," yawns Tracy.

"Yeah, I guess. But I didn't bring mine. Did you?" Fran replies.

"No," Tracy yawns again. "Here." She takes Fran's hand and pretends to "spell" a word in her palm, using the deaf alphabet, just as Annie Sullivan—Helen Keller's teacher—did for Helen when she was a little girl. Only she doesn't really know how to form the letters. Harriet Birnbaum told her to fake it—but make it look real. Fran and Tracy had both watched a famous old black-and-white movie about Helen Keller, which was based on the play, so they knew what the hand motions should look like. Both girls had cried at the end at the end of the movie, when Helen suddenly understands that the words Annie has been spelling into her hands actually mean something—a way of communicating with the rest of the world. The girls thought Annie was so brave, so smart, and so patient—and she was going blind herself! And to think the whole thing was a true story, too! "Bad girl!" Tracy pretends to spell into Fran's hand. Fran, in response, shuts her eyes and waves her head around, grunting. But the girls are too tired to do more.

"So," asks Tracy, yawning widely as a rerun of *Full House* fills up half the living room, "what should we do for your birthday this year? We've only got, like, three weeks to figure it out."

The girls have been planning each others' birthday parties since they were six, when Fran decided she wanted all her friends to dress like cowgirls, with fringed skirts and cowgirl hats with a leather drawstring under the chin. Unfortunately, it was too cold in February to rent a pony for pony rides, though Fran had begged and pleaded for one. Instead, she and Tracy drew and cut out horses using brown construction paper, and taped them up all over

Fran's living room. Carla had thought putting Scotch tape on the walls was a small price to pay for ending the pony ride debate.

Fran sinks back into the couch. She's exhausted, and it's not quite eleven o'clock. Maybe raising kids is harder than she thought. "I don't know," she yawns in reply. "Midnight bowling?"

"Maybe," replies Tracy. "Are you going to invite Mindy this year?"

"I don't know. I don't think so. Do you think I should?"

"No," Tracy replies. "She's really obnoxious. She's always going around talking about her Gucci this or her Chanel that. She's so, like, materialistic. It's like she doesn't think about anything else."

"Yeah, she's gotten sort of boring. What about Tayisha?"

"Definitely," Tracy replies. "She's very cool. She's really funny."

"So, we'll do pizza at my house, then midnight bowling at Bowl Around, and then cake back at my house? Then we'll crash?"

"Sounds good. OK," says Tracy. "And chocolate-chip pancakes for breakfast."

"My dad's specialty, as you know," says Fran. The pancakes were a birthday tradition for Fran. At Tracy's house, things ran a little differently. Her mom and dad had divorced when Tracy was four, and her mother had remarried two years later. Tracy liked her step-dad, but he related to her best when she agreed to go out and throw a football with him, or go ice skating, or swing a bat at his under-handed softball pitches. Cooking and baking were definitely not his thing. Tracy saw her real dad only one weekend a month, because he had moved to North Carolina after the divorce. She had no brothers and sisters. Tracy knew—and the Singers knew—that the Singers had long ago become a second family for her, stable and predictable. Fran thought her family was outrageously boring, but Tracy always felt safe and sound with the Singers, and she liked that feeling. Birthdays at Tracy's usually involved a large crew of noisy girls, a gigantic cake ordered from the bakery, and an envelope full of cash from her mother and step-father. The noise and hilarity generated by the birthday party was a gift in itself, for Tracy, to break the routine silence that penetrated her household.

Once Fran and Tracy finish the business of organizing Fran's party, and drawing up a guest list—including, it must be said, a long list of girls who would not be invited—
they sit watching old sit-com reruns and a show about rich girls throwing lavish Sweet 16 parties for themselves. They discuss everyone they know in great detail, and scout the kitchen for more goodies—but decide that they don't want to look greedy, after all. Finally, little by little, both girls nod off to sleep, sitting up on the soft gold-upholstered couches in the Vinings' living room. When the front door unlatches quietly around midnight, and Tonya and Fred walk in, the girls are flopped over on their sides, Tracy leaning unconsciously on Fran's shoulder.

Chapter 11

On the morning of Friday, February 11, Fran opens her eyes from a deep night's sleep and is instantly awake. Two completely unrelated thoughts crowd her consciousness. First, that she is officially a teenager, at last—well, technically, since about two-thirty in the morning—the time of her actual birth, according to her mother. And second, that she is deeply grateful that she didn't catch a terrible virus like Helen Keller did as a baby, causing her to lose her sight and hearing. Imagine having a birthday every year, and not being able to see your cake, see your friends, or watch and listen to everyone singing Happy Birthday? There were worse fates, sure, Fran figures—though she can't think of any off-hand. But that would be pretty desperate.

Fran flings off her covers and drops her feet to the icy floor. She pulls aside the curtain over the window seat, and exhales a warm breath onto the fogged windowpane. A fresh blanket of snow lies over the grass, dusts trees and branches, and makes everything look brand new. Even the old family Subaru parked in the driveway looks fresher, somehow. Fran can't help but think it was all done for her benefit—Nature's way of saying happy birthday. Then something catches her eye—an unfamiliar box lying on her desk. The box is small, wrapped in silver paper with a silver bow on top. A tiny card is attached. *From mom and dad, with love*, it says in her mother's handwriting. Fran snatches up the box and tears off the tiny wrapping. Inside is a tan leather box with a hinged lid, and gold lettering stamped on top. The letters spell the name of a local jewelry store—one that sells engagement and wedding rings. She's never been inside. Fran opens the box and inside a nest of white cotton lies a gold chain with a brilliant pale violet amethyst dangling from the end. Her birthstone. Fran knows right away it's the real thing—not a fake—not because her parents are snobs about this sort of thing, but because it's their way of acknowledging her new status. Fran knows this without even really thinking about it. She also knows it's about the most un-hip present she's ever gotten. Beautiful, sure, the way anything shiny is beautiful. But not cool like the chunky green beads she's seen on girls at school. It's so old-fashioned—like something a girl in an old historic romance novel would wear, she imagines. Still, she lifts the pendant out of the box, picking off a few strands of cotton as the chain uncoils, and fastens it around her neck. She checks the mirror. Not too shabby, actually. The amethyst hangs right in the hollow of her neck. Not really so un-cool, maybe. Fran thinks she's got some earrings that are about the same color—not amethysts, but they'd probably go well together. She decides she'll just keep it on, permanently. That will please her parents, she knows, and she can still keep the amethyst out of sight, most of the time, unless she wants it to show.

Unfortunately, it's still a school day. Fran dresses and heads downstairs for breakfast. Charlie's leg cast has only recently come off, and he's using a cane to support his weak leg. "Here she is, the teenager of the house!" Charlie says in a big hearty voice, hobbling over to her to plant a kiss on her forehead.

"Dad," says Fran, rolling her eyes. "Don't make such a big deal out of it. A lot of my friends have turned 13 already. It's not a world headline or anything."

"Yeah, Dad," says Toby, plucking toast from the toaster, and slathering it with grape jelly. "It's just an ordinary birthday. Jeez."

"So, Tobes, did you get me anything?" Fran asks, pulling the milk jug out of the fridge for a quick swig.

"No. I totally forgot. Sorry," Toby replies, sounding not the least bit regretful.

"So," asks Carla, after giving Fran a squeeze, "did you find—". Before she can finish, Fran pulls the necklace away from her collar, so her parents can see.

"It's a really pretty color," Fran says. "And I've already got earrings that match. Thanks a lot." Fran shakes off a flash of irritation. If only her mother weren't so quick to seek approval for the gift. Yeah, yeah, it's nice, what else is she going to say? Thanks, but actually it's really boring and I don't really want to wear it? Can't her mom just not make a big deal about it? Then she feels guilty—surely this was expensive. She wonders if her parents picked it out together, but when would they have done that?

"Lemme see," says Toby, coming over for a closer view. "Oh. It's just a boring necklace. What's the big deal?"

"It is a big deal," says Charlie, fumbling for his briefcase, a long tube of blueprints, and his cane. "This is our first teenager. Does this mean you're going to start randomly shouting and screaming about nothing?" he asks with a grin.

"Dad, she already does that," says Toby.

"Oh, now," says Carla. "Just wait til you're older, Toby—"

"I'm a boy, Mom," says Toby with exaggerated emphasis. "I'm not going to get all hysterical. Remember when Dad broke his leg? Fran was a basket case. She was yelling and screaming at me the whole time, after you left for the hospital."

"What?" says Fran, raising her voice. "I did not. I was cool as a cucumber. You are such a little liar." Fran reaches across to bat him one, but Toby moves out of her way just in time. "You little imp."

"It's time for the teenager and the imp to get to school. March," says Carla. For once, Fran is eager to get to school because she knows—or at least, she suspects—that Tracy and Tayisha and some of the other girls will wrap her locker in birthday paper—a school birthday tradition—and probably bring in all sorts of candy or cupcakes.

Friday passes in a pleasant haze, particularly once she's out the door and away from her hovering parents. Tracy and friends deliver on the wrapped locker and the treats—the presents will be delivered on Saturday, at the party. When Fran gets home, she finds that Tonya Vining has dropped off a present for her: it's a silver charm bracelet, with dangling moons and stars. Fran thinks it is really beautiful, and elegant, and it reflects her IM screen name—something Tonya couldn't have known. And she feels a pang of guilt, because she thinks it's more beautiful—and more cool—than the amethyst necklace her own parents gave her. But then, Tonya is so much more stylish than everyone else in the neighborhood, it's not surprising she'd know what to buy. The gift comes with a note: *To our beloved neighbor and the best babysitter in Baltimore. Fondly, Tonya, Frank, and Theo.* Fran is truly touched. And she laughs to herself, trying to imagine little Theo picking out a piece of jewelry. He'd probably drop it down a toilet or something, just for the pleasure of watching it sink to the bottom.

"Isn't that sweet," says Carla, when Fran shows her the bracelet. "You've really made out well in the jewelry department this year. You know what you have to do, right?"

"Duh, Mom," replies Fran. "Write a thank you note. I will. Tomorrow."

"Well, soon, anyway."

The Singers go out for dinner, as they always do when it is someone's birthday. Toby usually asks to go to Fuddruckers. Fran decides this year she wants Indian. She loves ordering *palak paneer*, partly because she loves the sound of it, and partly because she loves the combination of creamed spinach and cubed cheese, which sounds disgusting, but is actually quite delicious, especially when wrapped up in a piece of onion *kulcha*, which is like thick pita bread, served warm. Toby threatens not to come, so he doesn't have to eat that disgusting mush, but in the end, he really has no choice, so he comes along, eats nothing but rice, and sulks until the family returns home again, for a private celebration of cake and ice cream. Suddenly, Toby discovers his appetite and asks for a third piece of cake, which is denied. Stuffed, Fran keeps picking at the blue border of icing that rims the cake—a cake Carla did not have time to bake herself, as she was down at the real estate office most of the afternoon—but which was purchased from the kids' favorite bakery in town.

Saturday is dull and cold and dreary. It's a real day-after-birthday-day, a come down, a big anticlimax. Fran logs on to her Mac to IM about the evening's plans with anyone who happens to be on—which is practically everyone, on a cold, boring Saturday afternoon. "Everyone" means the girls Fran has grown up with; the crew who watched Barney together, and Sesame Street, and played ring-around-the-rosy, and learned to swim under water and ice skate and do ballet. That crew.

> franonstage: want to come over early? i'm bored stiff
> tracysouttahere: sorry, can't! got 2 go to stupid museum 2 c stupid paintings
> franonstage: tell them no
> tracysouttahere: can't say no. u know stanley. hard boss.
> dooronron: got u such a cool present, cant w8 2 c yr reaction
> franonstage: cool! cant w8!
> dooronron: is m coming
> franonstage: no
> dooronron: oh thank g-d. wh about g
> franonstage: which g...g__l or g__y
> dooronron: guess
> franonstage: g__y not coming
> dooronron: wh a relief
> cancantutu: want me to bring cd's or dvd's
> franonstage: sure, whatever u want
> nutmegspice: and i got u a poster of u know who
> franonstage: dont tell me, y r u telling me
> nutmegspice: so u can dream about him
> franonstage: ok i'm swooning, falling onto my bed. actually i'm starving, going 2 get lunch. ttyl

Fran's friends are scheduled to arrive around eight. Bowling doesn't start until ten. It's called midnight bowling because the lanes stay open very late on Saturday nights, and they turn on a whole stream of neon lights that bathe the bowling alley in a weird purple-blue glow. Every time someone nails a strike, a

88

series of strobe lights flicker across the alleys, temporarily blinding all the players, but no one seems to mind. There's a jukebox that blares old rock 'n roll, and a snack bar serving the usual junk—though the curly fries are exceptional, Fran and her friends agree. It goes without saying—and Fran and her friends don't say it—that bowling is totally dorky. But that's beside the point. Once you're actually doing it, it's fun. And the later it gets, the more fun it is. The bowling shoes they make you rent are totally disgusting, of course. The shoes look awful and sometimes they're sort of damp and sticky inside. But once you've had them on awhile, you sort of forget about it, and they do grip the lane, so you can throw the ball.

After a long afternoon that never seems to end, during which Fran studies a scene in *The Miracle Worker* that she knows she'll be rehearsing next week, and makes a half-hearted attempt to knock off some math problems, only to decide she can't do half of them without asking the teacher a question, which means the whole thing will have to wait until Monday. . . after all that, the party finally gets under way. Tracy arrives first, followed by Gail and Tayisha and Megan, and then finally Veronique (Ron to everyone) and Pilar. They form a noisy sea of blue jeans, flipflops of every stripe (never mind the cold, wet pavement that seeps through the bottom of the rubber) and zippered fleece sweatshirts. The girls hang out in Fran's room for awhile, while Toby bangs loudly on her closed door, just to annoy them. Fran decides she'll open presents after they come back to have cake. A heap of gift bags with fluffs of tissue paper sticking out, and boxes wrapped and beribboned, sit stacked on her desk. Sleeping bags and pillows are piled next to her bed. Then the girls move to the living room, where Carla puts out bowls of popcorn and pretzels; dinner will be eaten later at the bowling alley. Toby grazes from bowl to bowl, making sure to scoop up as much of the popcorn as he can.

"Mom!" Fran calls. "Will you please get Toby out of here?"

"Tobe," Carla says, "come on, leave the girls alone. Dad said he'll watch *Star Wars* with you until it's time to go, so why don't you go into the den." Toby leaves, but not before seizing a large handful of pretzels.

Once Fran and Tracy had settled on Bowl Around for the party, Fran quickly struck a deal with her parents. Since the place was nearly forty-five minutes from home, out in Columbia, a quick drop-off, with no parental units remaining behind, was out of the question. Neither Carla nor Charlie wanted to do that run twice in one night. So Fran agreed, reluctantly, to allow her parents and Toby to come—provided they took a lane as far away from Fran and her friends as possible, and didn't interfere with them all night, until it was time to leave. Money for food and drinks would be handed over in advance.

Once the girls are settled in, and they've all tied on their smelly bowling shoes, Ron volunteers to keep score for first game. Ron is always happiest when she's put in charge of something. As scorekeeper she could shout out the name of whoever's turn it was, and call all the plays. The others knew that Ron had a bossy streak, and usually they didn't mind indulging her, especially if it spared the rest of them to focus on something else, like gossip. Ron's booming voice always came as a big surprise, since she was a small girl with curly reddish-brown ringlets and dimples.

"Tay is up! Gail on deck! Tay, come on!" calls Ron, totally into the game. Tay and Gail and Meg are sitting on a pink plastic bench behind the scoring table, deep in conversation. Fran, Tracy, and Pilar are on the next bench over, their heads bent in conversation.

"He is not! Oh my God, you are so wrong!" says Gail, picking green nail polish off her index finger. "I saw him go in, and he wasn't, I swear!"

"Oh, Gail, you are so into him, it's not funny. Were you stalking, or what?" laughs Meg, squinting all around, because she refuses to wear her glasses.

"I was not! I was just there, on my way to the library!" replies Gail, blushing slightly.

"Yeah, right," says Meg, laughing.

"Tay!" calls Ron. "Let's hustle!"

"Don't tell anymore 'til I get back," Tay instructs Gail and Meg. "It's my turn." Tay is tall and thin with long arms and even longer legs. She lifts out a speckled brown bowling ball from the rack and takes aim.

"Whoa, a split!" calls Ron, dutifully marking the score sheet.

"I'll never get that," says Tay, eyeing the two pins that stand like sentries on opposite sides of the lane, and waiting to lift her second ball. "They're too far apart." Tay decides to aim for the bowling pin on the right—her balls always tend to curve in that direction, anyway. She misses both, her ball heading straight down the center.

"Gail, you're up!" calls Ron, as Tay turns away from her deadbeat ball and rolls her eyes. Gail throws a gutter ball, and then another. She waves at her second ball.

"Bye, bye, baby! See you later. Oh, well," she says, and returns to her seat on the bench.

Fran leaps up and bowls an eight—not too embarrassing. Pilar and Tracy each knock a few down, but not too many. Finally, it's Ron's turn. She puts her pencil in the little curved rim on the scoring table, so it won't roll away, and saunters over to the balls. She spits into the palms of her hands for good luck, and rubs them together.

"Eeww, Ron, that's disgusting," says Pilar. Pilar is the only girl not wearing jeans; instead, she wears a tight denim jean skirt that's been ripped on purpose, and purple tights.

"What, I saw somebody do that on TV once," says Ron. "I always wanted to try it. But yeah, it's disgusting, isn't it?" Ron lifts her ball up even with her eyes and takes aim. She brings her arm back slowly and lets it rip. The ball flies straight down the center of the aisle. .. it's a strike! Instantly, a bell starts clanging and bright white strobe lights start blinking rapidly, causing all the neon lights surrounding the bowling lanes to appear as brightly colored streaks of purple, red, and blue. The girls cheer.

"I want to do that!" says Tay. "Will you teach me?"

"I don't really know how I did it," laughs Ron. "I just did it."

"Let's celebrate!" says Fran. "Pizza and fries and milkshakes!" The girls abandon their half-played game to sit on bar stools at the snack bar.

"Oh, God, I love the curly fries here," says Tracy. "They're awesome."

"They make you break out, you know," says Pilar.

"Who cares?" replies Tracy. "It's worth it. I'll eat yours."

"Oh, no, you won't!" says Pilar.

The girls place their orders and hang out on the bar stools waiting. Suddenly, Fran does a double-take. She sees her mother at the far end of the snack bar—which runs almost the entire length of the bowling alley—talking to some guy she's never seen before. And he looks young. And big, huge, in fact—probably the tallest and widest person in the whole place. Yet he isn't fat, exactly, just massive. Who on earth?

"What is going on?" Fran says out loud.

"What?" asks Gail. "Oh my God, don't tell me he's here— you don't see—"

Fran laughs. "No, Miss One Track Mind. There's nobody here. My mom's just talking to somebody, that's all."

"Oh," says Gail, uninterested.

"Look," says Fran. "See that guy down at the end, next to my mother? He's huge, but he doesn't look very old, does he?"

"I can't see!" says Meg, squinting as usual. "Where?"

"You are so blind, Meg," says Tay. "Your eyes are all scrunched up—no wonder you can't see anything."

"Yeah," says Tracy. "I see him. He's giganto."

"Maybe your mother has taken a lover, Fran," says Pilar. "And they arranged to meet here, all innocent."

"Yeah, right," says Fran. "And *your* mother is jetting off to France with her boyfriend. Didn't I tell you?"

"OK, whose mother is likeliest to have an affair?" asks Gail, warming up to the subject now that it's taken an interesting turn.

"This is gross," says Ron, who could never imagine any man other than her father taking an interest—*that* kind of interest—in her plain and very plump mother. "Not mine. Not in a million years."

"Not mine, I hope," says Tracy. "She's already on her second guy. I don't need anymore father figures in my life."

"A lover isn't a father figure, Trace," says Meg.

"We know someone who's perfect for the job, don't we Trace?" says Fran.

"Oh, right, Tonya."

"Tonya—that's a perfect name for somebody having an affair," says Pilar, crossing her legs and swiveling on her bar stool.

"Yeah, but she's not," says Fran. "At least, I don't think so. She and Frank—that's her husband—they seem pretty into each other."

"Wish I could say the same for my parents," says Ron. "I think they just tolerate each other."

"Same," says Gail. "But at least they're nice about it. It would be awful if they were screaming and yelling at each other all the time."

"I think that's what happened between my mom and dad," says Tracy. "But I was too little to remember, really."

"This conversation is becoming a real downer," says Ron. "Hey, we're here to celebrate Fran's birthday, aren't we?" As if on cue, the girls' food arrives, and everyone digs into curly fries, burgers, and pizza.

By midnight, the girls admit they've had enough of bowling to last a year, at least. Ron gets a *second* strike, Tay gets one—which causes her to jump up and down screaming. And the rest of the girls get a lot of gutter balls and a few miscellaneous splits. Fran walks down to the far end of the bowling alley, to where Carla, Charlie, and Toby sit slumped in their plastic seats, their eyes glazed with fatigue. The remains of a pizza and fries sit perched on the side of the scoring table.

"OK," says Fran. "We're done."

"Thank God," says Carla. "We were about to haul you all away, anyhow. Toby's wiped, and so are we."

"I am not!" says Toby, rallying a bit. "Fran! I got a strike! It was so cool!"

"That's great, Tobe. I wondered whose that was, when the lights flickered."

"Let's go warm up the cars," says Charlie. He and Carla each had to drive, because one car isn't big enough to fit everyone. So the girls and Toby pile into the old Subaru or Charlie's Honda Civic and caravan back to the house. By the time the cars pull into the driveway, all the girls have drifted off, and Toby is out cold.

"OK, girls, everybody out of the pool," says Charlie. The girls stretch and yawn and shiver, and scoot into the warm house as quickly as possible.

"Dad," says Fran sleepily, as she gets out of the car. "Who was that guy Mom was talking to?"

"What guy?"

"The guy in the bowling alley. The big guy."

"Oh," says Charlie. "I think he's the relative of one of Mom's clients. She's trying to sell his mother's house, or something. I'm not quite sure. I think the mother is sick and her son is helping out. Something like that."

"Oh," says Fran. "Do you think she'll ever actually sell a house?"

"I don't know," Charlie chuckles. "We'll see. There's always a first time. Maybe this'll be the one."

Fran and her friends spread sleeping bags and pillows all over the living room floor—the furniture is pushed out of the way to give them more room.

"G'night, girls," says Carla, heading upstairs with Toby dragging behind her. "Don't stay up too late, and please, please, don't make too much noise."

"We won't," says Fran. Now that they're out of the warm, hypnotic rhythms of the car, the girls begin to rally. "Cake! Let's have cake!" says Fran.

"I'm dying for a piece of cake!" says Meg. And they all pile into the kitchen and fall on the chocolate cake with white icing and rosettes that's sitting on the counter.

"Wait!" says Tracy. "We didn't sing Happy Birthday." So the girls all whisper a hasty rendition of the song, and then dig in. They don't even bother with candles—which is fine with Fran, since she already played that game the night before with her family. Having her friends here, altogether, is enough. All in all, Fran thinks, it's been a pretty decent birthday.

Chapter 12

Fran is panting, and her brow is coated with sweat. She's getting a real workout—but this is way more fun than gym.

"OK, that was pretty good," says Harriet Birnbaum, looking up at the stage from the front row of seats, below. "I want you to run through it again. James—" she addresses Scott, who plays James, Helen Keller's adult half-brother, by his character's name, "I want to hear more dripping sarcasm. You're angry with your father and you're angry that Helen is allowed to run wild. Captain Keller, you're indignant. Let's hear it. This young whippersnapper, Annie Sullivan, has come into your house and practically taken over. She's interrupting your dinner and bossing you around." Captain Keller is played by a short, broad boy named Ben. He's shorter than his 'wife,' played by Carole—a girl who, in real life—would never actually hang out with Fran and Tracy, as she's more part of the mall-obsessed crowd. Fran and Tracy used to crack up over the difference in their heights, but now they're used to it, and Ben, though short, does have a surprisingly deep voice, which is good for Captain Keller to have.

"Annie," continues Harriet Birnbaum, looking at Tracy, who, like Fran, has been breathing hard and is red-faced with exertion. She takes off the dark round wire-frame sunglasses she's been wearing—Annie Sullivan had eye troubles, too, and was bothered by light. What kind of word is 'whippersnapper,' Tracy wonders briefly, blinking in the glare of the bald stage light. She can't imagine ever hearing let alone using that word again for the rest of her life. She glances over at Scott—she hasn't yet told Fran that she's been kind of crushing on him because he has a cute smile, but there isn't time to dwell on any of this at the moment. But Fran's already figured this out, anyway. "I liked that when you took Helen's arm and twisted it—keep doing that. And Helen,"

Harriet addresses Fran, "all the pent-up rage, frustration, and anxiety you can muster. You're like a wild horse that keeps throwing off its rider. You don't want to be tamed. OK, let's run it again."

The rehearsal has already lasted an hour and a half—the cast was excused from last period to work on the production—and they're all bone-tired. Even the tireless drama tyrant, Harriet, has been drinking from a giant cup of Starbucks coffee. But they're all really into it—and they know they've got a chance to make this really impressive. It's hard not to get caught up in the scene: This genteel, old-fashioned southern family, the Kellers, is trying to enjoy their mid-day dinner. The nineteen-year-old Annie Sullivan has only recently joined the family to work with Helen, and is appalled by the young girl's complete lack of table manners. Helen wanders around the table—blindly, of course— grabbing fistfuls of food from people's plates. This is at a time when people like the Kellers got all dressed up for dinner and put cloth napkins in their laps at every meal. Annie can't believe the Kellers put up with Helen's animal-like behavior, when manners are everything. Susie Nichols plays the other member of the family at the table, Aunt Kate. She's sort of a dimwit who doesn't really grasp what's going on around her—Aunt Kate, that is, not Susie, who's OK, but not great. She sort of overdoes the old-lady bit, Fran thinks. Tracy has Fran by the wrists, to keep her from grabbing any more food. The rehearsal props are limited: just a table and chairs, and a few paper plates. The grabbing is all imaginary, at this point. But for the real thing, Harriet said they'll actually set the table and put real food on the plates. Which means Fran and Tracy are going to get really, really messy. That's something to look forward to. Dress rehearsal is still three weeks away, however, and there's a lot to work on between now and then.

"OK, people, from the top," says Harriet.

KATE: *Miss Annie, you don't know the child well enough yet, she'll keep—*

ANNIE: I know an ordinary tantrum well enough, when I see one, and a badly spoiled child—

JAMES: Hear, hear.

Keller [very annoyed]: Miss Sullivan! You would have more understanding of your pupil if you had some pity in you. Now kindly do as I—

ANNIE: Pity? For this tyrant? The whole house turns on her whims, is there anything she wants she doesn't get?

Shortly after this point, Annie Sullivan persuades the family to leave the dining room—even Captain Keller. She and Helen then have a showdown, as Annie tries to teach Helen how to sit at the table, put a napkin in her lap, and use silverware to eat from her plate. Helen's never done this before—and she's not about to start now. Fran and Tracy have worked out all the moves, but they don't want the scene to look too mechanical, so they keep surprising each other with extra kicks, punches, wrist-grabs, and hair pulls. They don't really want to hurt each other—but they want to come as close as possible, so that the audience believes they're really involved in a power struggle. While this battle is going on, Scott, Ben, Susie, and Carole, are supposed to be offstage for most of this scene, but today they just stand to one side, fascinated by the action. Harriet calls out to Fran and Tracy as they play out the scene.

"Good! That's good! Now grab the chair, Helen, like you're holding on for dear life. Pull her away, Annie, good! OK….keep it up…good. Now Annie, throw the pitcher of water in Helen's face, to shock her….That's good. Remember, girls, there's going to be real water in there, so Helen, be prepared to get doused!"

As Fran reacts to the "shock" of the water, she puts her hands up to her chest and gasps.

"Oh, my God!" Fran cries. Tracy abruptly lets go of her.

"What's the matter?" Tracy asks, straightening up.

"My necklace! My amethyst!" Fran says. "It fell off! I've got to find it!"

"All right, all right," says Harriet, annoyed by the interruption. "Calm down. It's here somewhere. You'll have to take it off from now on, before rehearsal," says Harriet. "You shouldn't be wearing jewelry, anyway."

"I know," says Fran, "but it was a birthday present from my parents. I just got it a few days ago." Harriet is not particularly sympathetic.

"Well hurry up and find it then," she says.

All at once, Fran, Tracy, and the other four main cast members are all crawling around on the stage, looking for the necklace, and cracking up. Things have gotten a little intense, so they're secretly glad for the break.

"Oh, Captain Keller, we've got to stop meeting like this!" says Carole to Ben, in an exaggerated southern accent, as they meet under the rickety old folding table. Fran can't imagine flirting with Ben—which she knows means she must be superficial, since the only thing she has against him, really, is that he's short.

"Come here, my little honey," replies Ben, deepening his voice even further. "Give Daddy some sugar." Carole squeals and crawls away, forgetting all about the necklace.

"Annie! I do declare!" says Scott in a fake southern accent. "You have ruined this family! Simply ruined it!" Tracy laughs in response to this weak display of wittiness—a wee bit too much, Fran thinks, her own eyes glued to the floor as she searches. But then, Scott isn't really her cup of tea. Fran then lunges for the necklace, which sits harmlessly off to one side of the stage set, the gold chain curled in a coil.

"I found it! I got it!" says Fran. "Oh, God, what a relief." She sits on stage, holding the amethyst on its gold chain, inspecting it for any damage.

"All right," says Harriet. "Stick it in your backpack and let's finish the scene. And don't wear it to rehearsal again. That goes for the rest of you girls, too. No jewelry at rehearsal."

By the time five o'clock rolls around, Fran and Tracy are completely wrung out. They sit huddled in their coats on a bench in front of the circular drive that runs past the front door of Whitney Middle School. Tracy's mom is supposed to pick them up at five-fifteen.

"I can't believe we have a Spanish test tomorrow," says Fran. "I feel like crawling into bed as soon as I get home."

"I know. I have, like thirty math problems, too," says Tracy.

"Maybe we could convince our parents we're both getting the flu, and stay home tomorrow."

"No chance," says Tracy. "My mom would send me to school even with a high fever." And for no reason at all—except perhaps exhaustion, nerves made raw by the intense rehearsal, the shiver of damp winter air blowing across the campus—the girls crack up to the point of tears, which continue until, and even some minutes after, Tracy's mother pulls up and honks impatiently for them to pile in.

Chapter 13

The day of opening night arrives at last. Fran has nearly reached the point where even the name Helen makes her nauseous. And if she ever sees another pair of earplugs again, she may actually vomit. Fran and the rest of the cast are to remain at school on Friday; the curtain rises at eight in the evening. The day has been a complete waste for all of them, preoccupied as they are with the Big Night ahead. Math, Spanish, History—in one ear and out the other. Since getting the role of Helen, Fran's status at school has shifted a bit; it's not that she's got more friends, or even new friends. But everybody knows who she is, and even kids she barely knows nod as they pass in the hallway. It's kind of cool—and also maybe a bit of a burden. Fran has wondered if she's supposed to act differently, or do something different. But that's not really her style. She'd still rather hang out with Tracy, Gail, Meg, Ron, Tay, and Pilar than anybody else. Today, even the kids doing stage crew—mostly geeky guys who liked to hammer and saw a lot, or run the light board—are restless and getting a buzz of attention. Fran knows that Carla, Charlie, and Toby will not only be in the audience, but probably as close to front and center as they can get. Fran had hoped they'd sit way in the back of the auditorium, where she couldn't see them, but no such luck.

"Are you kidding?" Charlie had said a few days earlier, when Fran suggested, uselessly, that maybe her family didn't really want to come and see the play, it wasn't really such a big deal…. "I think we should get there at least half an hour early, so we can be sure to scout out the best seats."

"Yeah," said Toby. "I want to be close to the stage so I can watch you screw up! Hey, Fran, if you forget your lines, I could bring your script and read them to you!" Fran rolled her eyes and sighed.

"Thanks a bunch," she had replied sarcastically, "I'm not going to forget my lines. I'm sick of my lines, at this point."

"Yeah, but if you get really nervous, you might go completely blank, you know?" Toby offered. Naturally, this was Fran's biggest fear—the one that had kept her up worrying, more than a few nights running. But would she let Toby know that? Not if her life depended on it.

"Never mind him," Carla had said. "He's just goading you."

"I know, Mom," said Fran, impatiently.

"We promise not to distract you from the audience, right guys?" Carla looked directly at Charlie and Toby.

"Oh, no, no, we'd never do that," said Charlie, in an unconvincing tone—shooting Toby a look.

"Boys!" Fran shouted. "Give me some space!"

On Friday, Fran, Tracy, and the rest of the cast are too nervous to eat lunch. By six-thirty, though Fran has barely eaten all day, her stomach is in knots, and she can't even think about food, though big bags of cheese doodles, potato chips, and pretzels are sitting around backstage. Carole's mother, who has volunteered to help out before the Friday and Saturday night and Sunday matinee performances, helps Fran pull on her pinafore—the old-fashioned doll-like dress that Helen Keller wears. The dress fits over a tee shirt and shorts, and the back closes with Velcro, so it's easy to get into and out of. Fran already feels rivulets of sweat running down her back, despite the drafty, unheated air wafting around backstage behind the big, dusty velvet curtain, where cast members are milling about. There was no way Fran would let her own mother back here to do this—that's way too much to deal with.

"You're all set," says Carole's mom, smoothing down the Velcro closures. "Tracy, you're next." Tracy's cheeks already look flushed—as though she and "Helen" have already had their tussle in the dining room.

"Think what a mess we'll be by the end of the night," says Tracy, as Fran stands close by, watching her don a floor-length dress with puffed-up shoulders. The dark sunglasses worn by Annie slide into a pocket sewn into the dress. At Wednesday's full dress rehearsal, Fran and Tracy had both ended up covered in baked beans and tater tots—the foods Harriet Birnbaum had chosen for their excellent smear factor. Because the girls only have one costume each, Carole's mom will have to run over during a brief black-out between scenes and sponge the worst of the mess off of them. The audience will have to pretend they're wearing clean clothes after that, even if the brown baked bean stains remain.

Fifteen minutes before curtain time, Harriet gathers the entire cast together backstage, and has them all stand in a circle, their arms stretched across one another's shoulders. It's embarrassing—but by this point, emotions are running so high, it's impossible for anyone to figure out what they're feeling.

"I want everyone to take a deep breath," Harriet instructs. Fran thinks she seems tense, too, which is sort of funny. Usually, adults don't take things as seriously as kids do, Fran thinks, and Harriet always seems to show only one emotion about anything — steely determination—as far as Fran can tell. But maybe directing plays is her whole life, thinks Fran. I guess we're supposed to show off for her. "When you get onstage, I need you to forget all about the audience," Harriet continues. The cast snickers. "I know you can't really forget about them, but I mean I want you to go deep into your character, and really be in the moment, like we talked about all week. Can you all do that?" Everyone murmurs some sort of assent. "Good, OK. Well, good luck. And break a leg."

The circle breaks apart, and Ben and Carole take their places on the darkened stage, for their opening scene. Harriet retreats to a dark corner at stage right, next to the ropes that control the dusty velvet curtain. The house lights dim, a hush falls over the audience, and the curtain rises. It's time to perform *The Miracle Worker*. . . .

Suddenly, it seems, after no time at all, there's a commotion coming from the audience. People are on their feet, whistling, clapping. What? Then it hits Fran: That's it. We're done. Opening night is over. It will never come again. And then: Oh my God, we have to do this two more times. The cast members join hands on stage, in front of the curtain, as they've rehearsed. They link hands, then bow. The applause lasts through two rounds of bowing. No one takes a solo bow—not even Fran. Harriet Birnbaum had told them all she doesn't believe in a star system; everyone in the cast deserves the same professional consideration, she had said. Fran and Tracy and most of the others were impressed by this; if only their social lives could be so fair and just. Fran squints through the spotlights, trying to pick out familiar faces in the audience. Just about the entire seventh grade is here, and most of eighth, too. Fran realizes she's drenched in sweat and the stench of canned baked beans clings to her. She's grasping Tracy's clammy hand on one side, Ben's on the other. Tracy has managed to get Scott's hand, Fran notices—an odd thing to notice at a moment like this, but still, there it is. Then Harriet Birnbaum, wearing a black turtleneck sweater and a long black skirt, looking every inch the drama queen, steps out on stage and takes a deep bow as well. The crowd cheers some more. Harriet turns her back to the audience and faces the cast. She blows them all a smiling kiss—the kind of dramatic, emotional gesture none of them could have imagined her making even a day earlier, during the no-nonsense dress rehearsal. The cast members spontaneously applaud her. Fran knows, without having to ask, that each of them is realizing, at the exact same moment, what a debt of gratitude they owe to their pushy, almost irritable, drama teacher. It's been for this—always for this moment. And now, the moment is over—and Fran can't tell whether she's sorry or simply relieved. People are starting to grab coats and walk out into the aisles, though a few loud whistles and "Bravos!" can still be heard.

The opening night cast party, held in the teacher's lounge, which has been thrown open to visitors for just this one night of the year, passes by in a complete blur. Fran has hastily thrown on a pair of jeans and a dry tee shirt; Tracy and most of the rest of the cast have done the same. They've scrubbed off their stage makeup, and now face a seemingly endless stream of family and friends, each offering the same words: *Congratulations... This was the best play I've ever seen...You were awesome...Oh my God, I had no idea you were so talented...I really thought you were blind, how did you do that?..* Plates of cheese and crackers, cookies and juice, sit jumbled on tables where faculty members usually eat lunch or prepare lessons. All of the cast members fall onto the food, ravenous.

"Hey!" says Toby, grabbing a cookie from Fran's plate, since he couldn't get near the table. "That was pretty cool. Was she a real person?"

"Thanks," says Fran with a full mouth. "Yeah, Helen Keller was a real person. Guess I didn't need you to read me any of my lines," she says, chewing. While she's still eating, her parents each grab her for hugs and kisses, and to share all sorts of predictable compliments about how awesome she was, et cetera. Fran looks around to be sure nobody is witnessing this embarrassing public display of parental affection. But it seems other parents are busy doing the same to their kids. Fran looks across the noisy room in time to see a short, stocky man with his arm around Ben's shoulders, posing for a picture that Ben's mother, presumably, is taking with a digital camera. Fran can't figure out why you'd want a picture at a time like this. What does it matter? What are you going to do with it, anyway? Store it in a digital photo album with a caption? "The Night My Son Was In A Play." How lame is that?

Then Fran sees her mother speaking with Harriet Birnbaum. Fran can only hope that Harriet isn't saying anything to embarrass her. But chances are, she is, since Carla is nodding and beaming while Harriet talks. Fran leaves Toby by the cookie table and scouts around for Tracy, who's joking loudly with Carole and Scott.

"Oh my God," Carole is laughing hysterically. "Did you guys know that when we were at the table, pretending to eat those cruddy beans, Scott had his back to the audience and he was making these ridiculous faces? I was almost cracking up! Did you see that?"

"Scott! That is so cruel!" says Tracy, batting him on the arm. "I would've peed in my pants!"

"Are you gonna do that again tomorrow?" asks Fran, laughing. "Good thing I'm blind!"

"Mm, I don't know. I might," says Scott, grinning. "It's my goal to try and make Carole laugh at the worst possible moment."

"No!" laughs Carole, practically weeping. "No! Don't do that to me! I'm not going to look at you! Not once, the whole time!"

Fran watches Tracy to see if she's bummed out that Scott seems to be paying a whole lot of attention to Carole. But she doesn't really look bothered, so Fran decides she's not going to obsess over it. "Where are you parents?" Fran asks Tracy.

"Around, somewhere," Tracy waves. "They did the usual, you know, you were great, blah, blah. In their own quiet way."

"I'm sure they thought you were awesome," Fran says. "They just don't like to show it."

"Yeah, whatever," says Tracy, shrugging. "It's fine." Fran and Tracy are suddenly surrounded by squeals.

"There you are!" says Ron, with Meg and Pilar alongside her. "Oh my God, that was so amazing! You were both so amazing!" Ron is practically bouncing up and down, she seems so excited about the play.

"Really, it was awesome," adds Meg, in a quieter voice. "I don't think I could memorize all those lines."

"You get used to it," says Fran.

"Hey, what do you mean?" says Tracy. "You didn't have any lines!" The girls all laugh.

"Yeah, you're right. I guess I had it easy," Fran grins.

"Trace, can I see that dress you were wearing?" asks Pilar, who once again appears as the fashion-forward member of the group, in a cashmere twin set with jeweled buttons and low-slung designer jeans. "It was old-fashioned, but kinda cool. Retro, I guess."

"It's in a pile somewhere backstage," says Tracy. "I'll show you later. It probably smells, anyway."

"Hey, what was all that food you were throwing around?" asks Ron. "Was it real?"

"Oh, yeah, it was real!" says Fran, who has vowed never to eat tater tots again in her life, or kidney beans. Fran and Tracy answer a stream of questions from their friends—including a few seeking details on Ben and Scott—until all the refreshments have been eaten, and kids start trailing away with their parents.

Later that night, alone in her room—alone for the first time in what feels like forever, with no teachers around barking orders, no parents smothering her with emotion, no friends seeking her attention, complicity, or just plain sympathy—Fran is too wired and too tired to lie down. She takes a long hot shower, both to erase the sweat and grime from the Kellers and to try and wash away the residual tension that's got her all locked up and jangly. As she slips on a nightgown and brushes her teeth, Fran's mind is elsewhere—anywhere, really. One moment she's flashing back to a dramatic moment in the play, the moment, right near the end, where Helen suddenly grasps the connection between the water surging out of the pump and into her hands, and the symbols that Annie is pressing onto her palm. W-A-T-E-R. It's corny, all right, but that moment gets to Fran every time. And while she doesn't know for sure if it's true, it's supposed to be true, and so she chooses to believe it happened that way—as though, after being locked inside a deep, dark closet for the first several years of her life, Helen Keller suddenly was handed a key that allowed her to step out into fresh, warm sunlight. Then the scene fades and Fran restlessly throws herself into bed, thinking now of Tracy and the

107

emotional distance that seems to separate the members of her family—Tracy herself, her mother, and her step-father—to keep them from understanding one another, or perhaps even trusting one another. For as long as Fran has known Tracy, even when they were quite little, Tracy has seemed to want to keep her family as something apart from the rest of her life. Which is probably why, Fran realizes, Tracy has spent so much more time at Fran's house, than the other way around. For all her family's faults—and they could be as irritating as, well, as anything—Fran unconsciously thinks of them as a part of herself, not as something entirely separate. She never could, and would probably not want to, draw the kind of boundaries Tracy has drawn—whether to keep her parents away from the rest of her life as a girl, and now a teenager, or whether to keep herself as separate from them as possible, while still actually living under the same roof. Perhaps it's always been both, Fran thinks.

Before she quite realizes it, Fran is snuggling down beneath her quilt, her thick, damp hair spread out on the pillow. Her eyelids begin to flutter, and she can feel the last of the buzzing energy and tension from the long, long day draining out of her. And after a few more images flit across her mind's eye—Ben and Scott crawling around on the floor, looking for her necklace, Carole laughing hysterically backstage, her brother stuffing Oreos into his mouth in the teacher's lounge, as though they'd been put there just to satisfy his personal sugar cravings, and finally, the loud burst of applause that rose up out of the audience as the curtain rang down on the middle school premier of *The Miracle Worker*—Fran drifts off into a deep, exhausted, and reasonably satisfied sleep.

Chapter 14

The remaining two weekend performances of the play pass by in an energetic blur. The magic that Fran and the others had felt on opening night is never quite duplicated. And the audience shrinks with each performance. For the final performance, the Sunday matinee, the auditorium is barely half-filled, mostly with restless elementary school kids and their parents—friends and relatives of cast members or others in the community who had a reason to attend, or to be dragged into attending. Fran finds it's very hard to remain blind when scads of eight- and ten-year-olds are swinging their legs, chewing gum, whispering, or just basically acting distracted. On Sunday afternoon, when it's all over, Harriet Birnbaum hands each member of the cast a little gift box wrapped in gold paper with a gold bow. The girls are each given a gold pin with two drama mask faces—one happy, the other sad—attached to each other. The guys each get a ring—the kind of big, chunky ring guys buy as class rings in high school—with the same drama mask faces. Where Harriet got this stuff, Fran can't imagine. But everyone manages a big "thank you." Fran knows she'll be asked by her mother to write a thank you note, as well, though the verbal thanks are probably good enough for Harriet Birnbaum. Afterwards, Fran, Tracy, and Carole study their pins.

"So, are you actually going to wear this?" Carole asks, pursing her lips.

"Well," begins Fran.

"No, not really," adds Tracy. "But it's the thought that counts, right?"

"Right," the two girls reply, slipping their pins into their backpacks.

"Well, see you around," says Carole. The girls know full well they won't be hanging out together. Carole's in a different crowd—with kids who are louder and somehow pushier than Fran

109

and Tracy. Still, they all know they've been through something together, and there's sort of an unspoken bond. It's there with Scott and Ben, too, but that doesn't mean anything, really. Which is to say, nothing will come of it. Carole might continue flirting with Scott, but Tracy isn't likely to make a move in his direction, Fran guesses.

With the play over, and mid-term exams rapidly approaching, Fran hardly notices the approach of spring until one day, upon leaving school, she realizes all the bare trees show little light green leaves, and that it's time to shed her coat. She thinks, briefly, of all that's happened the first part of the year—and just before—with her dad breaking his leg in a scary skiing accident, the all-consuming play rehearsals, and the surprise of her mom, just last week, finally selling a house. Her first sale, after a year of trying. And tonight, even though Fran has lots of studying to do, they're all going out for Chinese food to celebrate.

"To the real estate woman of the year," says Charlie, lifting a water glass, once they've all settled into a semi-circular booth at the restaurant—a long-time family favorite, just a few miles from home in a suburban Baltimore strip mall. The restaurant doesn't look like much from the outside, but the kung pau chicken and the shrimp with cashew nuts taste great, every time. Even Toby likes the food here—though he orders the same lo mein dish over and over.

"Well," says Carla drily, "I don't think I'm quite ready for the real estate hall of fame. But you see, kids, there's a lesson here." Both Fran and Toby roll their eyes in a rare moment of sympathetic agreement. "If at first you don't succeed—"

"Yeah, we know," says Fran, "try, try again."

"But that's boring," says Toby. "I'd rather quit and try something else."

"But I didn't quit, Toby," says Carla, dipping her chopsticks expertly into a steaming plate of white rice. "That's the point."

110

"Whose house did you sell?" asks Fran, spearing broccoli with one chopstick—driving it right into the stalk. "And who bought it? Was it anybody from our neighborhood? Anybody we know?"

"I don't think so," says Carla. "Actually, I guess I just got lucky. A young man walked into the office one afternoon, when I was the only one there, and said he was trying to sell his mother's house, because she was so sick."

"Wait a minute, I've heard this before," says Fran. "Where did I hear this story?" Fran pauses, her chopsticks in mid-air.

"At your birthday party, at Bowl Around," says Charlie. "Remember that guy Mom was talking to?"

"The really big guy?" asks Fran.

"What big guy?" Toby asks.

"That big guy at the bowling alley," says Fran. "That's right. Dad said you were trying to sell his house, or something."

"I don't remember any of this," says Toby. "Nobody tells me anything in this family." He puts down his chopsticks and picks up a fork, in order to scoop a large bunch of lo mein.

"You mean you only just sold it?" asks Fran. "What took so long?" Charlie and Carla both laugh.

"Selling a house is a long, slow process," says Carla. "Sometimes it takes months and months. Besides, your birthday was barely two months ago. That's not a long time."

"Well how much money will you make?" Fran asks.

"My commission isn't very big, I'm afraid," says Carla. "It's a pretty small house, and I agreed to reduce my commission, because they're struggling, and the poor woman is so sick, and her son had to leave college to take care of her, and--"

"You're just an old softy," says Charlie, grinning. "Your mother will not be adding to our nest egg any time soon. But that's OK. Sometimes you do something for the challenge. Not everything is about money."

"I'm only going to do things I'm paid for, when I grow up," says Toby. "Nobody's getting anything for free."

111

"Is she going to die?" asks Fran.

"Who? The mother?" says Carla. "Yes, I think so. But Peter didn't exactly say so."

"That's so sad," says Fran. "Peter's the son? He's so gigantic, I didn't think of him as somebody in college."

"Boo hoo hoo, I think I'm gonna cry," says Toby in a fake-sad voice.

"Oh, shut up," says Fran. And on that note, the family finishes eating, and Fran, upon returning home, dives into a textbook chapter on President Franklin D. Roosevelt and World War II—not by choice, of course, but because there's a test on it tomorrow—

while Toby sneaks onto the computer in the kitchen alcove to play race car games against an invisible opponent.

Chapter 15

The sun is bright white and hot, and the noise of jackhammers is deafening. Fran feels awkward and out of place, and she's trying desperately to ignore the furtive stares boring into her, like hot lasers, of the work men in their yellow hard hats and filthy overalls. She hates the hard sat sitting heavily on top of her own head, pulling at her hair, and channeling hot sunlight directly into her scalp. But she wouldn't be allowed onto the construction site without one. Obviously, Fran is deciding, this was a really, really stupid idea. That's what boredom will get you, I guess, Fran thinks. If you're bored enough, any activity sounds better than none at all. School's been over for only ten days, summer has officially been launched, and already it feels like an eternity since the last half-day of classes. The two-week canoe trip Fran plans to take with Tracy, Pilar, Meg, and some of the other girls is still a month away. Theater camp doesn't start for two more weeks. And the family's annual summer trip to the Vermont cabin is eons away, in late August.

What's a girl to do with so much time on her hands? Gee, how about going to work with Dad at the construction site of a big new office complex that's going up on the west side of downtown? Hmm, clear views of the Baltimore harbor and sky line...a cool breeze from the tall building...lunch at a fancy downtown restaurant...sounds pretty good. A whole lot better, anyway, than sitting around at home, while practically everyone she knows is on a post-school holiday somewhere. Pilar was going to invite her along to Rehoboth Beach for a few days, but that fell through for some reason. And so here she is with Dad. Only it isn't any fun. The men are staring at her legs—it's hot, why shouldn't she wear shorts? Her dad is busy looking at huge sheets of construction plans with a bunch of guys wearing light blue short sleeve shirts

113

and ties. He's hardly had any time to take her around. All the men wear big, heavy steel-toed work boots, including her dad, which look funny with the shirts and ties. Charlie is wearing a plaid sport shirt and no tie. Fran isn't sure if this is a subtle sign that he's more important than everyone else, or maybe less important. Oh, well, it doesn't matter now.

"Sorry, pumpkin," Charlie calls over to her. "I'll just be another minute. Then I'll run you up in the elevator to the top floor, where they're laying down the electrical. And then we'll go have lunch, OK?" He flashes her an apologetic smile. When she was younger, that worked wonders. Today, though, Fran is just plain irritated. And hot. And resentful of the men who keep sneaking peeks at her. She knows they won't dare talk to her, because her father is standing close by. But still, she feels hemmed in.

The situation improves, slightly, once she and Charlie are finally riding up the construction elevator to the top of the building site. The ride is scary because the elevator is little more than an open steel platform powered by a hydraulic lift. The higher they go, the more exposed Fran feels—exposed to possibility that she could lose her balance and fall, plunging to certain death amid the steel beams and construction gear below. What would the work men do then, Fran wonders. Stare at her twisted body?

"Is this good?" Charlie asks, as they rise up above the ground-level heat and dust. "Look out there, you can see all the way to the Francis Scott Key Bridge. If it weren't for all the haze, you could see clear up the Susquehanna." Charlie sounds enthusiastic—and Fran knows he's not just putting it on for her. He loves this stuff—the process of building something, the noise and chaos, the ability to see things from an angle few get to share.

"Can I take off my hard hat up here?" Fran asks.

"No, you can't. You have to wear it everywhere on the site, even up here," Charlie says. "I saw one of those hats save a man's life, once." Fran perks up.

"You did? You never told me that story."

"There are lots of stories I've never told you. Some of them quite unpleasant. But this one had a happy ending. This guy was working about six stories up, I think this was a bank building we were doing outside Philadelphia," Charlie says, wiping his sleeve across his forehead. Fran notices his hands and nails are coated with dirt and dust. "Anyway, he was standing on a beam and he slipped, for some reason. I think maybe it had been raining, and water had seeped through a tarp onto some of the beams. So he fell two stories down, landing on his head and shoulder."

"Oh my God, what happened to him?" Fran asks, horrified by the image of the man tumbling down the hard bones of the building.

"It was amazing, actually. He separated his shoulder, which was very painful, but fixable. And he had a mild concussion. But the hard hat saved his life, I'm convinced. He would've cracked his skull open, otherwise. In fact, the hat had a big dent in it, afterwards. We were gonna throw it out, but he asked to keep it, as a souvenir."

Fran touches the top of her own hard hat, which is hot from the sun. She has a newfound respect for this uncomfortable and unfashionable headgear, and realizes it would be foolish to remove it, hundreds of feet above ground. The elevator stops and Charlie takes Fran firmly by the arm and leads her onto some kind of sturdy platform—at least they're not standing on a narrow beam. From here, Fran can see through the summer haze way out into the bay. Sailboats dot the water—dozens of them. And Fran can see, but not hear, several motorboats streaking and bouncing across the water, leaving a trail of wake behind them. From up here, the city of Baltimore, with gleaming office buildings and hotels lining the waterfront, looks like a place to have fun. Along the walkways that line the Inner Harbor, thousands of families and tourists appear as color moving dots, strolling leisurely among the shops and restaurants.

"So, was it worth it?" Charlie asks.

"Yeah," Fran concedes. "This is beautiful. And it's a lot cooler up here."

"Always is," Charlie says. "Sometimes, if we're not too busy, I bring my lunch or a cup of coffee up to the highest floor of whatever building we're working on, just to catch a breeze and a view."

"Speaking of lunch," says Fran, "I'm starving. And really thirsty." Charlie leads them carefully back onto the elevator for the descent. After a few more words with some of the work crew, the two of them walk along one of the old cobblestoned side streets of downtown Baltimore, and into an air conditioned Japanese restaurant, where Fran gorges on cool sushi and downs a pitcher of ice water.

Later, at home, rung out from the heat and noise of the day, Fran plops down in front of the television. She's got a summer reading list to tackle—but that can wait. The summer stretches before her long and slow. Toby is playing at a friend's house, so there's peace and quiet, for once.

"So, how did it go?" Carla asks, peering up from paperwork she's doing at the dining room table. Stacks of fat folders marked Coldspring Realty are spread out on the table. Fran just doesn't get the real estate business. What does it involve, really? And what's all the paper for? You sell your house, somebody pays you, and that's that. What's the big deal? Her dad's work seems some much more transparent: Somebody agrees to pay to put up a big building on a lot somewhere, and a bunch of skilled work men—and some women, Fran supposes—get together and build it, supervised by people like her dad.

"Fine," says Fran. "No big deal. The views from the top of the building were kind of cool." Another *Full House* rerun is on, which is about to absorb all of Fran's attention.

"Mmm, good," says Carla, distracted by the contents of a folder she's reviewing. "Tonya called. She wants you to babysit Theo all day on Friday. What do you think?"

"What?" asks Fran, her eyes glued to the TV. "Theo? Yeah, good, whatever."

"So you don't have other plans for Friday?"

"Mmm, no. I don't have any plans. I've got nothing to do and nowhere to go all week."

"OK," says Carla. "Then call Tonya and tell her you'll come over Friday around ten. All right?"

"Mmm, fine," says Fran.

It's not until eleven-thirty that night, when Fran is fooling around online, that she realizes she forgot to call Tonya and tell her she could come over on Friday. But no matter, tomorrow is Thursday. She could tell her then. Tonya always knew she could count on Fran, and Theo would have a whole day to get excited about it.

Chapter 16

"Fwan!" Theo bounds toward Fran as soon as the front door opens. Beautiful Theo, Fran thinks, what a long day lies ahead of us. What on earth am I going to do with you all day?

"Hi, Theo," Fran says, taking his eager little hand in hers. "Where's Mommy?"

"Here I am," says Tonya, stepping into the front hallway. "Thank you so much for doing this, Fran. I've got an all-day conference downtown, and I'd just be lost without you." Fran wonders what the conference is about—what kind of things interest Tonya Vining—but Theo is tugging on her tee shirt and begging her to play, though she's only been in the house for two minutes. Tonya is wearing a beautiful yellow sundress with a deep v-neck. She carries a short, cream-colored cashmere sweater over her arm. Her slim, tanned legs look elegant in a pair of strappy sandals. Must be a pretty fancy conference, Fran thinks. "These hotel conference rooms are just so cold, I hope I don't regret going with bare legs," Tonya says, talking over Theo's insistent chatter.

"Let's see," Tonya continues. "There's not much I need to tell you. There's all sorts of stuff for lunch in the fridge. You know Theo will be happy with a peanut butter and jelly sandwich. There's some iced tea, too, if you get hot and thirsty—running around with him, who wouldn't?"

"I've never been with him for a whole day. Does he nap?" Fran asks, trying not to sound hopeful.

"Unfortunately, no. You might get him to have some quiet time, with a book, but that's about it, I'm afraid. Are you sure this is OK?"

"Oh, yeah, it's no problem. I was just wondering."

"OK. Well, I should be home around four-thirty or so. And I'll call to check in when I can. Frank's out of town, so you shouldn't expect to hear from him." Tonya looks at her watch. "I've got to fly." She scoops Theo up and plants wet kisses on both his cheeks. "Bye, bye, sweetheart. Be good for Fran. Mommy will be home later."

"Mommy!" Theo yells. "Bye-bye, Mommy!" He hugs her legs and then runs in a circle around Tonya and Fran. Fran takes Theo's hand and they walk out onto the driveway together, to wave goodbye to Tonya as she slides into her silver Audi—the only Audi in the neighborhood. Everyone always knows when one of the Vinings is driving down the street in that car.

"Oh, and Fran," Tonya calls, as she begins to back down the driveway. "The pool gate is locked. You can play in the side yard, but just stay out of the pool area. You know."

"Yeah, of course," Fran calls back. "Bye, have fun. Wave to Mommy, Theo. Wave bye-bye." Theo waves and then runs onto the grass in the front yard and begins rolling around on it, like a happy puppy. Tonya has barely rounded the corner before Theo starts trying to climb the Japanese maple tree in the front yard. The small tree has low branches, and even though Theo is too small to reach them, he tries to shimmy himself up so he can grab the first branch. Fran sees no harm in letting him try—perhaps he'll actually tire himself out that way.

"Go ahead, Theo, climb the tree, you can do it," she encourages him. Theo pauses to consider her encouragement, then renews his effort to reach the lowest branch. But, as Fran had guessed, he's still too little. "Wanna play ball?" Theo gives up on the tree and runs to get his wiffle ball and bat, which are lying on the grass near the house. Fran pitches and Theo swings. He misses several in a row, then—more by chance than by skill—the yellow plastic bat connects with the wiffle ball, which goes sailing across the yard, clear over to the neighbor's hedge.

"Good job, Theo!" Fran says. "Now quick, go get the ball!" Theo darts away on his sturdy little legs to retrieve the ball. The game goes on for what seems like forever, to Fran. Sometimes Theo hits one, but mainly, he misses, his little body spinning around with the force of his swing. After this game, and some catch, and then a limited game of hide-and-seek—there aren't many places to hide in this placid front yard, Fran decides— it's finally time for lunch. They go inside and she checks the kitchen clock: eleven-thirty. Ninety minutes have passed since she arrived. With several more hours to go. It's a little early for lunch, maybe, but Theo probably doesn't care. Fran sits him town at the kitchen table with a set of crayons and a coloring book, so she can make sandwiches. But Theo isn't having any of it: instead, he opens a low cabinet where the Vinings keep dozens of neatly stacked plastic storage containers, and begins pulling them all out onto the kitchen floor, so he can build a tower. Fran figures there's no harm in this—though she knows she'll have to make time later, somehow, to restack and store all the containers. She doesn't want Tonya to come home and find the house in shambles—she might think Fran couldn't control Theo. That's not true. Well, not quite true, anyway.

"Here ya go, buddy," says Fran, putting down a plastic plate shaped like a football, containing a sandwich. She pours a glass of milk into a plastic cup, to go with it. Fran grabs some cheese out of the fridge for herself. No wonder Tonya Vining is so slim: there's just no time to eat when Theo is awake. "C'mon, Theo, sit at the table, please." She lifts him away from the containers and he climbs into a chair, on his knees. He takes a few bites of his sandwich and a gulp of milk, then climbs down again, sandwich in hand. Fran isn't sure if she's supposed to enforce table manners, or just let him wander. As long as she eats, he figures, he'll be happy. Theo goes back to his container stack, then wanders with his sandwich into the den, to play with his trains. Fran sees, with horror, that he's getting grape jelly on everything: the white door frame leading into the den, Thomas the Tank Engine, and his shirt. How did that happen? It was a simple sandwich, for God's sake. She runs to the kitchen to get a damp paper towel, but upon her return, Toby has climbed onto the back of the couch to reach for that glass ornament he likes so much. By now, bits of bread crumbs and more jelly smears have gotten onto the couch, as well. Clean up will have to wait.

"Theo, no! Climb down from there! You're being a bad boy!" Fran's voice sounds harsher than she intended. Theo looks at her, startled, and his face starts to crumple. "Oh, sweetie, I'm sorry," Fran rushes to him and lifts him off the couch, hugging him. "I didn't mean to yell, Theo. I'm sorry. But you know you're not supposed to do that. And you got jelly all over Mommy's furniture." Just then, the phone rings. It's Carla.

"Hi, honey, how's it going? Is he giving you any trouble?"

"No, Mom, everything's great. I've got it all under control. Theo is just, you know, Theo. He's eating lunch right now." She doesn't tell her mother that he's eating lunch all over the house.

"Good, honey. I know he's a handful. Just keep him occupied and you'll both be fine."

"I know, I am. I will. Look, Mom, I gotta go, he's banging his trains around and everything—"

"OK, honey. I'll see you later this afternoon, then. Bye."

Fran and Theo play trains for awhile, making the usual choo-choo noises. Theo decides to run his train cars not just on the stretch of track that's on the floor, but also across all the furniture. He knocks off all the loose couch pillows in the process, as well as a few knickknacks—none of which breaks, fortunately. More picking up to do, Fran notes. She realizes she hasn't even had time to straighten up the kitchen. In addition to the containers all over the floor, the peanut butter and jelly jars are sitting open on the counter, alongside a loaf of bread and a block of cheese. This is feeling more and more like *The Cat in the Hat*, Fran thinks. Theo is the mischievous Cat, who comes into the house when the mother is away and makes a complete and utter mess of everything. And the two innocent kids—she can't remember their names—can't pick up after the Cat fast enough.

Finally, Fran decides that the place Theo can do the least harm is outside. First, they make a trip to the potty, just to be safe. She doesn't know how much advanced warning Theo would give, when the time came, so better to get it out of the way. Then they head out through the wide screened French doors at the back of the living room that the Vinings installed when they had the pool built. The doors let in lots of light, giving the living room a cheerful summer glow, and there's a good view of the aqua pool shimmering in the light. A long silver and blue padded float with a built-in pillow drifts lazily around the pool. Fran wishes she could put on a suit and just lie on that float, as Tonya must do sometimes, when Theo is somehow occupied or asleep, and close her eyes and just glide on the pool's gentle eddies. But duty calls. The Vinings have installed a small swing set in a corner of the backyard, not far from the pool gate. Theo climbs onto the black-sling swing and begins rocking his body back and forth.

"No, Theo, like this," she says, and sits in the swing next to him. "Kick your legs out like this," she demonstrates, pumping her legs. "And it makes you go back and forth. You can go higher this way." Theo imitates her movement and begins to build some momentum. He laughs.

"Push me, Fwan!"

"OK, I will. But first try doing it yourself. That's right. Move your legs together, at the same time." Fran wonders if this requires more coordination than a three-year-old can muster, but he seems to be getting the hang of it. Then Fran hears the phone ringing inside; it's a good thing she left the screen doors open to hear it. "Theo, keep swinging. Do NOT get off. I'll be right back." She runs inside to grab the phone, and immediately begins walking back outside with the cordless, so that she doesn't lose sight of Theo. He's swinging and singing a song.

"Hokey-pokey! Hokey-pokey!" he sings happily, tunelessly.

"Hi, Fran," says Tonya on the other end. "How are you holding up?"

"Great. Theo had a sandwich and now we're on the swings. I'm standing right out back, watching him while we talk." She wouldn't want Tonya to think, for an instant, that she had turned her back on the baby.

"Oh, I'm so glad. I have such complete confidence in you. Things are going well here. I'm still on schedule, though I might get back just a little sooner than I thought."

"OK. Well, we'll see you later, then. Have fun."

Oh, boy, Fran thinks, putting the receiver down on the back patio. I've got to get the house cleaned up before she gets back. In the Vinings house, nothing is every out of place and you never see a speck of dirt. So that must be important to them. What would Tonya think if she walked in and saw grape jelly on the wall and the kitchen and living room a complete mess? Fran wishes she could call a friend for backup, but there's just nobody around. Seems everybody has beach plans or they're off visiting relatives, or they're away at camp. Even Tracy, good old reliable Tracy, has been dragged away by her parents to visit cousins in Chicago. What Fran wouldn't give right now to have Tracy here, helping out, laughing at the Cat in the Hat disguised as a little boy, and just generally lending moral support during the longest afternoon on record. There's always Mom—but no. And it's hot, too, Fran suddenly realizes. Blisteringly hot. It must be ninety in the sun, now. Maybe it's time to get Theo to come in for a cold drink.

Theo has left the swing and has begun climbing a knotted rope that dangles from the top of the swing set. The thick knots in the rope are intended as footholds, to help kids climb to the top—all seven feet or so. Theo is better at this than tree climbing. He's on the third knot by the time Fran reaches him. The cold drink will have to wait.

"Good job, Theo! What a good climber you are! Make sure you hold on tight while you're climbing." She stands alongside the rope, figuring she can spot him if he begins to slip—though if Theo really were to fall on her, she knows they'd both go down like lead weights. When he gets to the top, his head about even with the top rail of the swing set, Theo laughs.

"Fwan, look! I'm big! I'm bigger than you!"

123

"That's right, Theo, you are. Keep holding on, though. Don't let go. Do you know how to climb down?" Fran sees then that Theo has no idea how to reverse his moves. But he doesn't seem to care. Maybe he figures he'll just stay up there, a baby giant, forever. "Here, I'll come up and help you." Fran begins climbing but can't figure out how to maintain her own hold on the rope while helping him at the same time. Suddenly, she's worried he's going to get tired and simply let go. She pictures him falling to the ground, banging his head or breaking a leg. A slow panic begins creeping through her. "Theo, you have to come down now," she says, keeping her voice even. "Don't move, I'll help you." But how? She reaches up and puts her hand on his left ankle. "Theo, bring your foot down gently, to this knot underneath you." She tries to lift his foot off the knot; after several seconds, he cooperates and lifts his ankle. She guides it gently down onto the knot. "OK, now put your hands a little bit lower, like this." She demonstrates by moving her own hands down, one at a time. Theo begins moving both hands off the rope. "No, Theo! Wait! One hand at a time, see?" She shows him again. Her stomach is doing loops—and she again pictures him, as clearly as if it has already happened—falling backwards off the rope. But he gets it, and little by little, she coaxes him into reversing each of his moves. By the time he's reaching the bottom knot, Fran is back on solid ground and she grabs him around the waist and pulls him away. He resists.

"No! Me do it! Fwan, let go!" He squirms. Fran figures all danger has passed. He's only about a foot off the ground; he can get himself down. Fran exhales loudly; she hadn't realized she'd been holding her breath. And sweat is pouring off her. Theo, who is oblivious, and doesn't seem capable of sensing danger, lands safely, returns to the swing for about a minute, and then takes off again, running across the lawn. He's heading for a safe piece of equipment, Fran sees with relief—a hammock suspended between two oak trees at the back of the yard. Maybe…is it possible? If she rocks him in it, will he take a nap? Probably not, but it's worth a try, she decides.

"C'mon, I'll give you a ride in the hammock. Would you like that?"

"Yes," says Toby, pulling down the lip of the hammock so he can climb in. Fran gives his bottom a push.

"Rock a bye, baby, in the tree top," Fran sings, watching him. Theo sits up, clutching the sides of the hammock.

"Higher!"

"This isn't the swing, Theo. It doesn't go so high." But she pushes him hard, so the hammock swings in a wide arc. She pushes the hammock as far as it will go, without spilling its contents.

"Wheee!" says Theo gleefully. Then she slows it way down. "Dizzy!"

"Try lying down," Fran tells him. "And close your eyes. That'll stop the dizzies."

"Dizzy!" says Theo again. He lies on his back and shuts his eyes, perhaps to see what kind of thrill he can get from this angle, Fran thinks, rather than simply to comply with her wishes. He begins singing hokey-pokey again. Then Fran hears—yes, she really does hear it—a yawn. She peers over the edge of the hammock. Theo is lying with his eyes closed, smiling. She knows he's not sleeping—but he's still. That's something. She checks her watch: two-thirty already. Where did the afternoon go? Tonya could be home in an hour or so, and the house still needs cleaning up.

"Theo," Fran says softly. "You lie right here. Nice and still. Listen to the nice birdies singing in the trees. I'm going to run inside for two minutes." She watches for his reaction. He's actually lying quite still, and his eyelids seem to be fluttering. Is it possible? Fran steps away quietly from the hammock and stands watching for a moment, to see what happens. No movement. The hammock is still swaying slightly. She steps forward and gives it another gentle push. Still no movement from within. She walks backwards toward the house, keeping an eye on the hammock, until she is satisfied that Theo may actually have drifted off, lulled by the heat and the motion of the hammock. It's the first time he's been still, truly still, all day; no wonder he's tired, Fran thinks. When he wakes up, we'll have a snack and maybe play some more wiffle ball.

Inside, Fran gets busy. She puts away all the food, and wipes down all the counters and the kitchen table. She notices Theo had spilled milk on the floor, so she wipes that up too. Then she wipes off each of the plastic containers—he got jelly on those too—and stacks them neatly inside the cabinet, taking care to nest each one inside its larger neighbor. Before heading to the living room, Fran glances out back: No sign of Theo, which must mean he's still in the hammock. So far so good. Fran takes a damp rag and begins wiping jelly off the living room doorway. Then she brushes all the sandwich crumbs off the couch, straightens all the pillows, and organizes Theo's train set. From the kitchen, she gets a mini-vacuum and returns to the living room to suck up crumbs. Not exactly how I thought I'd spend my summer vacation, Fran thinks, vacuuming. But Tonya will be impressed when she comes home, to see how well I've managed every thing. Maybe one day, if I ask her, she would take me shopping for new clothes. She has such amazing taste. I bet she knows stores my mother never heard of, Fran muses, scouting the living room for additional crumbs and stains. She finds a small blot of grape jelly on the rug, and dabs it with a damp cloth.

Fran does one more walk-through of the downstairs, to be sure everything is back where it belongs, and that all signs of a hyperactive three-year-old have been erased—within reason. That wasn't so bad, Fran thinks. The clean-up took less than fifteen minutes. She returns the vacuum and drapes the rag over the sink, and then heads out back. She looks toward the hammock; it's still. She doesn't see Toby elsewhere in the yard. Could he really and truly be napping? She heads toward the hammock, but then something over by the pool catches her eye. There had only been one float in the pool, Fran could swear. Now it looks like there are two. The sun glare coming off the pool is intense; rays of white light are reflecting off the water into her eyes. Fran puts her hand up to shield her eyes. Yes, there are two things floating in the pool. How curious. She moves closer. No. No. This isn't what she's seeing. No. It's something else. Theo is in the hammock. Where else would he be? The pool gate is still locked. Fran leans over the gate, staring into the pool. She stands, staring, for what seems like an hour. It's like staring at a jigsaw puzzle where the pieces just don't fit. She can't figure out what she's looking at. What? What is it?

Part III

Fall, 2005

Chapter 17

There are thin, black cracks on my bedroom ceiling. They look like ski trails. Long, winding, dangerous ski trails. I would like to try running my skis along them. If I fell, or simply dropped into a bottomless ice ravine, it wouldn't matter. My ceiling has become my friend. I don't care if that sounds strange. I like the ski trails. They never change. On my ceiling, it is always. . .White. Winter. Stillness.

They have been giving me medicine. They think I don't know what it's for but of course I do.

But they never give me the only medicine I really want. The only one I would swallow with gladness. A Forgetting Pill. A Backwards Rewind Pill. A pill to turn me into Helen Keller. Blind. Deaf. Disconnected from all the sights and sounds that hurt so much. So very much.

But I can never have what I want. The only thing I want. The only thing, it seems, I have ever wanted in my whole life.

So I will instead lie here on my bed, looking up at the ceiling. It's what I do best now. It's really the only thing *to* do.

I don't know *what* to do. I don't know how to live, anymore. Funny, isn't it? Living is something I used to take for granted. Everyone does. You just get up in the morning and breathe, eat, speak, laugh. I don't do that now. So I guess I'm not really living.

What am I doing, then?

I haven't figured it out.

Chapter 18

They want to get me a tutor. For school. For school at home. Mom and Dad told me they thought it would help with my Recovery. That's a word I hear a lot, now, Recovery. Like it's some big, undiscovered country that we're all going to explore together.

The thing is, I've been Excused From School. For the whole year. I don't really know who put that deal together. There's a lot that goes on now, that I don't know about. And I don't want to know. Truth is, I don't have the energy to care, anyway. I just do what I'm told, now, basically. I eat when I'm told, if I can manage it. Mom reminds me to shower, if I forget, and I do it. So when Mom and Dad said they had hired a tutor to meet with me four days a week, so that I could keep up with my classmates, I just nodded. School used to be the biggest thing in my life. But lately, I haven't given it a thought. Heck, half the time, I don't even know what day it is. I probably couldn't keep track of a regular school day, even if I wanted to.

"What do you think, Fran? Does that seem like a good idea?" Mom had asked me, looking at me with those deep, new worry lines that had appeared between her eyes.

"The thing is, pumpkin, we want you to begin to regain a sense of normalcy," Dad added, placing his rough, calloused hand over mine. "This might be a way to do that. Slowly, of course. And at your own pace."

"And this way, you keep your privacy," said Mom. "We know that's important now. We know you wouldn't want—"

"Yeah, OK. Whatever," I replied, turning away. I did not want to hear anymore. "I'll do it." I could tell that Mom and Dad were relieved. Almost happy. Maybe they think this is going to make a difference. As if.

131

Chapter 19

"Hi."

This big hulking guy with shaggy hair, in a black tee shirt, holds out his enormous hand, the size of a steak, for me to shake. I look at it, but do not take it. This guy must be six-five, at least, and weigh 300 pounds. His shoulders are the size of couch pillows. I've been sitting in the den, staring into space. I have a vague idea I'm supposed to be somewhere else, doing something. But I can't remember what it is. It's a Tuesday, I think, though maybe it's Monday. Around two in the afternoon. The doorbell rings. Mom answers it; I hear her whispering. I'm used to that: hearing whispers all around me. Day and night. Sometimes the whispers are real, and I know they're about me. I don't know why they bother to whisper. Other times, the whispers are just in my head. Ugly whispers that I try to ignore. When I was in the hospital, right after the—well, right after the thing happened—there was whispering all the time. Inside of me, all around me. I couldn't always tell which was which. It didn't matter. I'm not sure it matters now, either. But I'm better at telling them apart. For what it's worth.

"She's in here, Peter," says Mom. "Fran, this is Peter. Peter, Fran. Peter is the young man I told you about, Fran. I sold his mother's house, when she was ill, remember?" I nod vaguely. Mom stands there, looking all white and tight, somehow. Peter reaches for my hand and shakes it. I guess he could crush it, if he wanted to. "So," says Mom, in an obviously fake cheerful voice. "I'm going to leave you two to get acquainted. I have some files to review. I'll just be in the dining room." I don't think Mom is into the real estate thing so much anymore, since she seems to be spending most of her time worrying about me, and watching me like a hawk, but it's as good an excuse as any.

After Mom leaves the room, Peter just stands there with his arms crossed. He looks like the President's bodyguard, or something. Except he isn't threatening, or frowning. And he's not packing any heat, as far as I can tell. He's got almost no expression, really. And he doesn't seem all that interested in chatting. Which is surprising—and a relief. I figured he'd be like all the other people I've met recently: ever so eager to chat me up, learn all about me, figure me out, prod me, advise me, sympathize with me, warn me. Whatever.

"So," I say after a couple of minutes of total silence. "What're we supposed to do?"

"What do you think we should do?" Peter asks, standing there like a giant statue. I shrug.

"How should I know? You're supposed to have an agenda, aren't you? I'm just the maimed girl who's ducking school."

"Maimed?" Peter asks. "How so?" This throws me completely. I assume Peter knows my whole sad story. That he knows the entire plot of my own personal horror movie. I turn away. "I thought we were going to study European history, algebra, *Hamlet*," he says. "No?" I shrug again, my back to him. "OK, well," he says.

"I don't know if I can concentrate on any of that stuff," I say, still looking away from him. I'm staring at the flower pattern on the back of a wing chair—a chair we've had forever, my whole life, probably. Looking at that pattern, a bunch of red and yellow flowers with twisting green stems and leaves, occupies my mind. Fills me up so there's no room for anything else. Where would I fit algebra, if my head is full of patterned flowers printed on fabric?

"In my experience, concentration isn't something you do. It's something you are," Peter says.

"Huh?" I don't understand a word he's saying. I don't care, either. But I'm trying, really trying, to be polite because it's what my parents expect. And I can't afford to let them down any more, ever, not even just a tiny bit. You know how your parents always tell you they love you unconditionally, no matter what. Well, I don't want to push the limits any further than I already have. I expect Peter to clarify his remark. But he doesn't. He just sits down in the flowered wing chair—lowers his bulk, I should say—and puts his head on his chin.

I watch him. This behavior doesn't seem quite normal. Which is refreshing. I'm the only one around here who hasn't been behaving normally. So it's good to watch somebody else act all freaky, for a change. Peter has brown hair that flops down into his face, and green eyes that never seem to blink. He wears old Reebok sneakers—at least, they look old, all ripped up along the seams, like a dog had chewed them. Who is this guy? What were my parents thinking? Should I be left alone with him?

"Are you a shrink?" I ask.

"No," he says quietly. "I'm only twenty. I'd have to go to medical school for a couple of years first."

"Are you in college?" Asking questions makes me so tired. It's not like I care. But he's sitting there, not doing anything.

"I was." I wait for him to continue, but he doesn't. I decide not to follow up. It takes too much energy. "I left," he says after another full minute of silence. He hasn't moved a muscle. I've never seen anyone able to sit so still. Toby will never be able to do that, I'm sure. I can't, either. The closest I get is lying on my back on my bed, staring at the ceiling. But then, there's no company around to get up and move for, anyway. "At least for awhile."

This conversation, if you can call it that, has moved so slowly, I can't remember what it's about. I yawn. Maybe he'll take the hint and leave. We don't seem to be getting any work done.

"I'm going to leave, now," says Peter. (Finally, I think.) "But I'm going to come back. Tomorrow. Is that all right with you?"

"Yeah, sure, I guess," I shrug a third time. Do I have a choice? Do I even care?

"Are you going to bring some books or papers, or something?"

"We'll see."

"Isn't that the point?" I'm growing a little impatient, now, with this guy who seems to be wasting my time, not that I don't have plenty of time to waste. But that's none of his business.

"Ah, the point. The point is something. . . we can talk about it tomorrow," Peter says. He rises from the chair and shows himself to the front door. He slips out without another word to me, or to Mom. I immediately go and find her in the kitchen, sitting in the alcove on the computer.

"OK, what gives," I say.

"What do you mean?" she asks.

"This Peter guy. What is going on? Mom, do you even know him? He's really, really weird. And you want him to tutor me? I don't think he even knows what time it is."

"You know, it's strange," Mom says. "For some reason, I really trust him. I really do. I can't explain it exactly. Maybe it was watching him go through this stuff with his mother. The way he handled it. He has a sort of quietness..." She stops abruptly and shoots a glance at me. "Well, I don't know. Anyway, all we ask is that you give him a chance."

"What does Dad think?" I ask. "And what about his mother? You mean she died? Do you think you can't mention death around me? Do you think I'll become hysterical? I won't. Don't worry. It doesn't work like that."

"I didn't think—"

"Anyway, this whole set-up is just stupid."

"Fran, it's just that you're not ready—"

"I know I'm not ready! I'm not ready for anything, anymore! I'm not ready to leave the house! Or read a book! Or laugh out loud! So don't tell me I'm not ready! I know I'm not ready! I'm not even ready to—to—"

"To what?" asks Mom softly, putting her arms around me. I'm shaking so hard I'm causing her to shake, too. Moments pass. I don't know how many. When I look up, her cheeks are wet, and so are mine. "Oh, baby," she says, holding me. "My poor baby. I want so much to make you better. I wish I knew how." I break away from her, gently.

"You can't. It's not your fault."

The kitchen door opens and Toby bursts in, tramping leaves and mud all over the floor.

"I'm starving!" he yells. "What can I eat?" Then he sees Mom and me, red-faced, our eyes all red. And he freezes. I can see that he just doesn't know what to do. I feel so badly for him. He's a casualty, too—and it's all my fault, of course. A house full of walking wounded. I may as well have set off a bomb in the living room. At least that way, the damage would be quick. "Never mind," he says. I can hear the anger in his voice—mixed with fear, and frustration, and anxiety. Maybe I can't really hear all that, but I know that's what he's feeling. He looks like a small bull ready to charge at the nearest object—maybe me. He drops his backpack on the kitchen floor and dashes up the back stairs to his room.

"Toby!" Mom calls after him. "It's OK! You can have a snack. Come back." Instead of chasing after him, she slumps onto a stool. "I don't know," she says, shaking her head and looking towards the floor. "I just don't know what to do, anymore."

"That makes two of us," I reply, bitterly.

Chapter 20

No matter what I say to him, or don't say, Peter shows up. He looms in the doorway, sweeping in cold, windy air. And then he finds me in the den, as usual. Waiting. And not waiting. Waiting means you're expecting something, or someone. And that means you care. And caring hurts. It hurts much, much too much. This much I've learned. So I try to wait without actually waiting. Peter says this is a good thing. I don't tell him any of this; he just seems to figure stuff out. He puts into words ideas you might have, that you don't even know how to put into words yourself. Ideas that sort of float at the back of your brain, like transparent ghosts gliding across a haunted room.

"When you're waiting for something," he says, sitting in the old flowered wing chair, in that still way he has, "it means you're trying to avoid the present and jump to the future."

"But that's impossible," I say testily. "You can't skip through time."

"No, but you can focus on different points in time. By waiting—and thinking about the fact that you're waiting—you're focusing on the future, on what's to come."

"So?"

"So, if you were able to truly live in the present moment, to accept *now* for exactly what it is, and not be anticipating anything else…"

"Well, what?" I say, not really following the conversation.

"Well, you'd be happy."

"You're kidding."

"No, I'm not."

"You're telling me that I, me personally, I could be happy if I lived my whole life in the present moment, and never thought about or expected anything from the future?"

"More or less, yes."

"Even if I could do that—and I can't—it would be horrible. How could dwelling on every moment, when you feel like you're always about to explode into a thousand pieces—how could that make me happy?" I get up off the couch and begin pacing. Peter has this effect on me. He upsets me, all the time. Yet it's a different kind of upset—different enough from the way I've been upset, for months, that it's almost a relief. Sort of like scratching an itch that's been driving you crazy—like the way Dad's leg itched when he had the cast on. But still, I hate this idea of living in the present moment, when every moment is so awful.

Peter doesn't reply. Instead, he opens a book he has brought—one of several—and reads:

When faced with pain and misfortune, simply stop and center yourself in the present moment, here and now; take a deep breath, sit down and concentrate.

"What does that mean?" I ask.

"In a way, it means that all the comfort you need, all the answers you seek, are already contained within your own mind." I give him a blank look. He leafs through his book and reads another passage:

To find the answers to your life questions, you must look within. Nothing less will do. Nothing more is needed.

I shake my head vigorously. "I don't know what you're talking about. Maybe you should go." I continue pacing the length of the den. "What is all this crap, anyway?" I'm practically shouting at him now.

"Have you ever heard of Zen? Or Zen Buddhism?" Peter asks, raising his eyebrows just slightly.

"Yeah, I've heard of it. We had a unit on world religions last year. I didn't pay much attention, though, 'cause I'm not, you know, a believer. I guess I'm an atheist."

"That's beside the point," Peter says. "The practice of Zen isn't about God."

"Well, what's it got to do with anything? What's it got to do with me? Why aren't we learning the stuff from school I'm supposed to know?"

"We'll get to that, Fran. Don't worry about it right now."

"Have you discussed all this with my parents?"

"No, I haven't, Fran." Peter looks at me expectantly. I nod slowly. He knows, and I know, that I'm unlikely to tell them a thing. These daily sessions have become my own private time and space, somehow; it's just about the only time of the day when Mom or Dad isn't crowding me, and Toby's not conspicuously walking around on tiptoes. So I figure I can handle this any way I want. And I just don't feel like playing by the rules, anymore. Look where it's gotten me, after all.

"May I continue?" Peter asks.

"I guess so. I've go nothing else to do," I say, rather bitterly.

"Zen is all about letting go."

"Of what?"

"Of everything you're fighting—everything inside you that is at war."

"What do you mean? How?"

"Through Zen, we learn how to pull our own poison arrows out."

When Peter says this, I stop pacing. I am full of poison arrows: I'd never thought of it like this before. But he's right. He's exactly right: That's what it feels like. Like I've been shot with poison arrows, and the poison is festering inside me. And I can't seem to get rid of it. To cleanse my system, somehow.

"How do you do this?" I ask. I don't really believe there's anything Peter can say, or anything I can do, that's going to help. But still. . . .

"Well, partly through changing the way you think about yourself, in relation to the rest of the world. And partly through meditation."

"Medication?"

"No. Meditation."

"You mean, like chanting?"

"Not exactly. Look, let's try something. Sit here, on the rug, and cross your legs." I do as he asks, mainly because there's no reason not to. Peter sits opposite me. He looks like a giant Buddha statue, with his legs crossed. "Just relax your hands in your lap. Close your eyes, and start breathing slowly and deeply—not too deeply or you'll hyperventilate. Focus on your breathing; listen to it. Feel it." Peter's quiet voice is lulling me. I don't believe in this meditation junk, but I have to admit there is something relaxing about just sitting here, breathing deeply. "Keep focusing on your breathing. . . that's good. . . .Now let your mind drift." I stiffen, and my eyes fly open. Letting my mind drift is a very bad idea: I'm likely to go places, mentally, that I don't want to go. There are images I've struggled for months to cut out—like a cancer that festers, making you sicker and sicker.

"Peter, I don't want to think," I say, in a warning tone.

"I'm not asking you to think. I'm asking you to stop thinking. Let your mind take you anywhere."

"No," I resist, still sitting cross-legged on the floor. He continues, anyway.

"When thoughts come, Fran, don't repress or hate them. Just notice them."

Just by saying this, Peter has opened up the gates of Hell. Images flash through my mind. Terrible images. Bright sunlight glinting off water. A metal gate. The flashing red light of an ambulance—red lights everywhere, and the blaring, deafening bleating horn that signals death and destruction. A stretcher with a small body all covered in white.

"No!" I yell, scrambling up from the floor. My heart is racing wildly. I can hardly catch my breath. "Get out!" I yell. "Get out! Leave! Go away! I don't want you here!" No one is home to hear me. Only Peter. I feel his shadow rising over me. He's murmuring something, gripping me in his big, bear-like arms. The noises in my head are so loud, I can't hear him. I force myself to think of Helen Keller: Deaf. Blind. I hear no evil. See no evil. But I do, I do. I can't control it. I am filled with poisoned arrows, and I don't know how to remove them.

Chapter 21

When I was in the hospital—it must have been late June or early July, everything is fuzzy from that period—I overhead a medical student tell a nurse that they had decided I wasn't suicidal.

Now isn't that good news, I thought to myself, lying in my white-sheeted hospital bed on the psych ward. I was placed in some unit or something where they put all the suicidally depressed, anorexic, psychotic, schizophrenic, murderous, drug-crazed adolescents. I wasn't any of those. I didn't fit in, really, which is funny in a sick sort of way, if you think about it. If you didn't fit in on the psych ward, my God, where did you fit in?

What got me there were the fits. I mean, what else would you call uncontrollable episodes of shaking, vomiting, hyperventilating, and screaming your lungs out in the middle of the night? I'd call that a fit. I don't know when they started—at some point after the initial shock wore off, I guess. When reality broke through and slammed me against the wall, knocking the breath out of me. Let's put it another way: When Tracy came home from her trip to Chicago to visit me. She walked into the house and I knew that she knew what had happened. At first, I thought it was going to be OK—or sort of OK. She hugged me tight.

"Oh, Fran," she whispered. "Oh, God."

But then something happened that I never saw coming. Tracy backed away from me, and turned away.

"I know," I said to her. "I know."

"No, you don't know," she said. "You were perfect. Everything about you was perfect. Your family was perfect. You, and Carla, and Charlie, and Toby—you were all like rocks to me. Do you understand?" Tracy was nearly shouting at me. A lump rose in my throat, and the room started spinning.

"What are you saying?" I asked her, weakly.

"I'm saying," she gulped, "I'm saying, you've—you've destroyed everything that was good—" I felt my knees begin crumpling under me, and reached out for a chair to break my fall. "You've taken something away—something that you took for granted. You got careless, or you didn't care enough, and you just threw it all away. And now, things can never be the same again!" Tracy was screaming at me now. "I came over because I thought I could handle it—but I can't!"

"How—" I stammered.

"This was *my* family, too, Fran! This was my home, too! Don't you get that? I was always safe here. I don't know how I'd have gotten through these last couple of years without you all. 'Cause I sure as hell don't get it at home."

Tracy came over to me and shook my shoulders.

"Look, I'm sorry for you!" she shouted. "I really am! But you had it all—and now it's all nothing. It's all horrible. And it— we—will never be the same again."

Tracy burst into tears. I was crying, too, now, really hard. My parents came running up to my bedroom, having heard the commotion through my door.

"Fran?" said Dad, walking quickly into my room. "What's happening? What's wrong?" I couldn't look at him—or Tracy, or anyone. I just fell to the floor. After that, I only remember bits and pieces. I don't know when Tracy left, or if she said anything to my parents. All I know is, it's over. She was here, beside me, always a part of me. And now she's not.

That must have happened, oh, two months ago. Maybe more. As I've said, I'm no good at keeping track of time. But it doesn't matter when it happened; it is still happening, inside me, every waking minute—and sometimes in my sleep, too. So Peter thinks I'm going to sit and shut my eyes and let my thoughts run where they may? Clearly, he understands nothing about me. When Peter comes today—and he is coming, I'm sure, despite what has passed between us—I am ready for him. I tell him, I am a

143

murderess, did you know that? I have killed two people. He looks at me quizzically, but, typically, says nothing, waiting for me to go on. My best friend, I tell him, I killed our friendship. I didn't mean to, but I did. So she is dead to me. I'll never see her again—or not on purpose, anyway.

"But there is always time," he says, watching me pace.

"Time for what? For playing scenes over and over in my head? Horrible scenes? Time for what, Peter?"

"Time for things to change. For you to change, and Tracy." I snort, disgusted.

"You don't know anything about it."

"Nothing is permanent," Peter says. "Everything changes. Always. Your consciousness is constantly shifting, changing. The present—the pain you feel in the present—changes as each present moment changes." I shake my head in bewilderment. My state is permanent; of that I am sure.

"No," I continue to shake my head.

"Fran, do you want to feel tortured your whole life? To let your demons control you, and never feel a moment's peace? Is that what you want?"

"Of course not," I retort. I want the poisoned arrows to come out. "But that's the way it is. I made my bed, now I have to lie in it. I'm a worthless piece of—" Peter reaches across to me and gently places his hand over my mouth.

"Don't ever, ever say that about yourself. Ever," he says. "I want to try to help you, give you hope, help you find some peace, but you must trust me."

"I don't even know you."

"OK," he says. "What do you want to know?"

"Why are you here?"

"I took a year off from school to help my mother. She was in so much pain. It was just the two of us. She adopted me, by herself, when I was an infant. So we always looked after each other. After she died, I withdrew from school because I wasn't ready to go back. Just like you. I met your mother when I was trying to sell our house—and when I found out what had happened, I told your parents I thought I might be able to help."

"Do they think we're just studying history, or something?"

"I'm not sure what they think. But they trust me. And I hope by now, you do, too."

"And all the Zen Buddhism stuff?"

"I'm a student of Zen and Zazen—that's the meditation part. I'm working on it. It makes sense to me. I'll be working on it my whole life, I'm sure. There's still a great deal I don't understand."

"Well, it makes no sense to me."

"That's understandable. So let me guide you. Look at it this way: You probably couldn't feel any worse than you do now. So isn't it possible that trying something new, something different, that just might help you feel a little better, is worth a chance?"

"Maybe. I don't know." I feel so tired, all of a sudden. Like I've been rolling a big rock up a mountain for days on end, and I can't even see the top of the mountain. My shoulders actually ache. Maybe it's tension, fatigue. I don't know. But I'm not sure I can fight it anymore—the terrifying nightmares, the feeling that I don't belong in normal society, anymore. The loneliness. And Peter— he's so sure, so persistent. Maybe it's time to give in. To give up. He's right about one thing: I can't imagine things getting any worse. "What do you want me to do?" I ask, wearily.

Peter asks me once again to sit on the floor and close my eyes. I immediately feel my heart begin to race—but I can't fight it anymore, either. It's like climbing onto the most wild and dangerous rollercoaster in the world—you don't really want to take the ride, but you do anyway, and brace yourself to be terrified and breathless. Peter begins speaking softly.

"Bring your attention to your breath," he says. "Feel the rise and fall of your belly as you breathe in and out. Follow the inhalations and exhalations for a few minutes. . . . Now begin to focus on your breath as you breath out. . . . Feel the air going out and dissolving into the space around you."

It's not as bad as I feared, I think to myself. If you really think just about the breathing, you can keep other things away. And that's good. But I really have to concentrate to achieve this.

"Now I'm going to teach you a little poem," Peter says. "I want you to remember it, and say it to yourself when you're alone. Listen, but don't stop breathing, and stay focused on your breath going in and out.

When suffering overwhelms me,
I will breathe in
And leave an opening in this moment
For the joy that lies just behind it."

I don't know why or how, but after he says this little poem, in a quiet, sing-song kind of voice, for a split second—so quickly, it is gone before I can fully register it—I am at peace. And if there is any way I can capture more moments like that—I will settle for mere seconds—I know I've got to try.

Chapter 22

The air has turned sharply colder. I can smell it, even in the house. I wrap myself in old, loose sweaters full of holes. I shuffle from room to room, like an old lady. Maybe this is what I will be like, as an old lady: Shuffling around, pulling my sweater tighter, thinking gloomy thoughts. Sunshine, laughter, the way friends giggle at nothing—all faded, pleasant memories.

But perhaps it will not be that way. Perhaps—I don't know. But today, I feel a tiny ray of hope. I did not have The Dream last night. I did not wake up screaming. And the cracks on my ceiling—I no longer wish to focus on them so much. I suppose you could call that progress.

Last week, Peter brought me a big brown pillow, to sit on when I meditate. It sits in a corner of my bedroom. I have been trying to do as he asked—trying because it seems to be the only thing that brings a little relief. Sitting with my eyes closed, focusing on the breathing…shutting out absolutely everything else. This is incredibly hard work—much harder than you would think. But it is like exercising. I find that the harder I try, and the more I try, the more I am able to turn into the breathing. I mean, to shut out the whole world, and all the pain that's in it—in me—and just breathe.

What a relief, to just be. If only every moment could be like that.

Today is Thanksgiving. And though it is only seven-thirty in the morning, I hear Mom stirring in the kitchen, opening cabinets and clanging pots. Still in my pajamas, I sit on the pillow, cross my legs and close my eyes. This doesn't always work. Some days are better than others. I try to remember some of the ideas Peter has taught me, to help me focus on breathing and meditating.

I remember something he told me yesterday, about feeling as though there are steel bands around your heart.

"See these bonds lessening, dissolving," Peter had told me, during our session. "Feel your heart opening, and know that it can do so slowly, at the pace it chooses."

I want to open my heart again—to remember that I have a warm, beating heart that pumps blood through my body, helps neurons fire in my brain, and gives me the strength to walk, stand, run, swim, skate…ski.

I want to live.

"Well," says Dad, heartily. "This is quite a beautiful site. I hardly know where to begin." The dining room table has been cleared of folders and is covered with a white tablecloth and the good silver. A roasted turkey sits in the center of the table, flanked by tall white candles and too many serving dishes filled with food: yams, mashed potatoes, green beans, glazed carrots, stuffing, and gravy.

"Whoa," says Toby, pulling out a chair, "who's going to eat all this?" As usual, he hasn't been anywhere near the kitchen while the hard work was going on, but he's here, ready to eat.

"I just thought we shouldn't cheat ourselves," says Mom. "It is still Thanksgiving, whether we're four or forty."

Mom has done all this, almost single-handedly, because it is a normal thing to do. We all know that. No one is actually fooled into thinking otherwise. I glance away from the food and toward the dining room windows, which send back a wavering reflection of the lit candles on the table. It is gray and gloomy outside, and the wind is howling. Inside, there's warmth, light, and the only people left who really love me—or at least, agree to tolerate me. I am aching to be happy. To tear off a drumstick and let the meat and the salt and the juice fill me up, warm me all over. The cold helps me remember that the sweltering heat and agony of the summer are well behind us now.

148

"Well, what are we waiting for?" I ask, trying as hard as I can.

"Aunt Syl?" asks Toby, grinning.

"No, no, not that," says Dad, putting his hands in front of his face, as if to ward off evil. "No extras this year, thank God. Isn't it nice for a change? Just the four of us? And think of all the leftovers! We'll be feasting for days!"

"Sit," says Mom quickly, to ward off the emptiness that wants to swallow up the whole room like a hungry, uninvited guest.

"I kind of miss Grandpa, though," says Toby.

"You do?" I say, surprised. The blind old man hardly ever says a word, it seems.

"You do?" echoes Dad.

"Yeah, he always gives me stuff, and he tells me amazing stories about when he was in the war, and how bombs were going off all around him, and stuff, and how he rescued his buddy."

"Does he?" says Dad, sounding pleased. "I never knew that. I'd forgotten. He fought in Korea."

"He never told me any stories," I say. "He just squeezes my hand and then leaves me alone."

"Your grandfather has always been partial to boys," says Mom, giving Dad a knowing look. "And he's old-fashioned about things like that. He doesn't know about equality between men and women."

"You mean women's lib?" asks Toby, helping himself to enormous portions of everything. "Pass the gravy, please."

"What do you know about women's lib?" I ask, forcing down a spoonful of mashed potatoes. They do taste good: I will try even harder. I reach for a drumstick.

PART III

Winter 2008

Chapter 23

The green light on the answering machine is blinking rapidly. It's the first thing I notice when we all walk back into the house, and easy to see in the cold, dark kitchen. If the house could speak, I think, heading for the machine, it would say, 'Not you again!' and tell us it was sick and tired of all the irritated mutterings, the angry stomping up the back stairs, the tear-stained pillows. Mom's haggard, hounded expression. And Dad's fake and determined cheerfulness. Enough already, our house would say. Lighten up.

I had always wondered what the word 'bittersweet' really meant. Not the chocolate kind—that was easy—but in relation to emotions. Now I finally knew. Skiing in Vermont this year had been bittersweet. Bitter and sweet. Hard and easy. Sad and liberating. I remember—it's stored in my bones, somehow—how free I felt on the slopes. I'm hoping that some day, after I die, if reincarnation is for real, I can come back to Earth as a bird—a big bird, with a six-foot wingspan. That would be way more fun than returning as, I don't know, a Zen Buddhist teacher. Then the view from the ski lift—with all the people in colorful ski gear below, and the white-topped mountains off in the distance—would be mine every day. Or whenever I wanted. And I wouldn't need much of anything else—a little food, a nest. Maybe a few chicks to feed. But that's it. There would be no boundaries: I could cross lands, seas, day, night. Time and space would be open to me.

Control is freedom. This much I know now.

Though the Dartmouth Skiway was more packed than ever this year, I was alone at the top of the Pine Ridge trail. As I dug my poles into the crusty snow, there was nothing but the icy rush of air, the *sshhhusshh* of my skis, as I slalomed down, down, losing my bird's eye view with every yard of descent. Somehow I couldn't picture Cynthia, Leo, or Katie out there. It probably wouldn't have worked, anyway. There's only one friend I was able to share this with, so easily—and it didn't matter that she couldn't really ski. I miss her so much—but now she's out of reach, swallowed up by the same big black hole I've fallen into. Only just like the real black holes in outer space, once you fall in, you can't see anybody else, or communicate with them, either. It's just big, black, empty—gaping, really—and cold. So it was Toby's turn this year: He brought his friend Sam. They were like a pair of Labrador puppies. Sloppy, excitable, running all over, tripping over their big feet. Noisy, and constantly hungry. I avoided them as much as possible, burying my nose in a book or a game of solitaire. The life of the party, that was me all right. At the cabin, the boys pressed buttons on their electronic toys, hauled firewood for Dad, slurped big mugs of hot chocolate. It was all very cozy. In a forced sort of way.

I press 'play' on the answering machine. There are two new messages. I know neither of them is Tracy; it's impossible, though a corner of me holds out a ridiculous hope that she'll forgive me. That she'll have called to say she's coming right over, that vacation has been so boring without me. And then she'd just walk through the kitchen door, like she never left, and we'd go up to my room and be bored together, leafing through *People* or IMing our friends.

No, one message is from Sam's parents, thanking us again for having him in Vermont. They must have called right after we dropped him off, less than half an hour ago. The other message is for me:

Fran, hi, it's Cynthia. I hope your vacation is going well. Hope you didn't break a leg skiing in Vermont. Anyway, I'm calling to invite you to a New Year's Eve party. I'm not sure when you're getting back, but if you're here, come to my house around nine. Everyone will be here, including You Know Who. It should be fun. OK, bye...Oh, tell your parents, my parents will be home and there won't be any alcohol. OK, bye, see you.

Unfortunately, while this message is playing back, my whole family is listening—and they're not even pretending not to. They're just standing there, still in ski jackets, with suitcases and ski poles dumped all over the kitchen floor. Toby is eating a granola bar he pulled from the drawer that never runs out.

"Soooo," says Dad, dragging out the syllable. "Who, might I ask, is You Know Who?" He peels off his ski jacket, but keeps his eyes on me, his eyebrows raised.

"Dad, come on," I say, disgusted.

"Charlie, leave her alone," says Mom, offering unexpected support. "She's entitled to some privacy." I'm not really all that grateful because I know exactly what Mom is thinking: That this must be about a BOY and isn't it wonderful I'm getting interested in BOYS because it means I'm MUCH BETTER and looking toward the FUTURE.

"I know who it is," sings Toby, in a teasing voice.

"You do not," I say, angrily, "and it's none of your business."

"Toby, lay off," says Dad in a warning voice—a big shift from his earlier tone.

"It's nothing, anyway. I don't know what she's talking about," I add. "So back off," I say to the family in general, and head up to my room, dragging my suitcase with me.

"Fran," Mom calls after me. Oh, God, not one more word of kind and protective encouragement, please. I don't think I can stand it. I can fend for myself in this family. "I want you to pull out all your dirty clothes and throw them in the washer tonight. You're back at school on Monday and I don't want you leaving it all until the last minute."

Well what do you know, I think. She's actually nagging me. Is that a good sign? I think it is. It means the gloves are off. About time, too.

I show up at Cynthia's door on Friday night, New Year's Eve, wearing the fourth outfit I had tried on since noon. I can't

153

wear what I wore to the dance last fall, that's out of the question. And I don't have much else to work with. As a last resort, I have borrowed an off-the-shoulder powder blue cashmere sweater from Mom (she started pulling all sorts of hideous things out of her closet and laying them out for me, but I put a stop to that as quickly as possible). I paired the sweater with a black skirt that I cut about four inches so that it's short enough to be presentable. The hem is a little ragged now, but I don't care. I have to hope I don't look too, I don't know, preppy. I was going to wrap my French braid, but decided that was over the top, so I left it to dangle down my back. So I'm hoping too that I don't look too young, or schoolgirlish. Or that I'm wearing too much makeup. Or too little.

All of this races through my mind as I ring the doorbell at Cynthia's house, after a quick drop-off. She lives outside my regular neighborhood, so I'm unfamiliar with these streets, two towns over, which are lined with old brick rowhouses with little front porches and marble steps. Nobody I know now lives close by; it's like I'm always striking out for foreign territory. It's not like walking around the corner to Tracy's, or half a block down the street one way to Pilar's, another way to Meg's, or Ron's. It's strange to think that all these other people have been around here all the time, doing their own thing, and that only as a result of circumstances—difficult circumstances, impossible, really—have I come into their orbit at all. And there are still plenty of days when I feel like I'm in nobody's orbit at all. . . just drifting by myself out into deep space. The really odd thing, though, is how I never run into any of my old friends, anymore. Where did they go? What do they do now? Do they miss me? And do I still miss them?

"Fran! Oh my God, you look amazing. Come in!" Cynthia has flung open the front door and has swiftly pulled my coat off my shoulders, before I can even shake off the cold January air—or my thoughts from a past life.

"Oh my God, Cynthia, *you* look really amazing! Where did you get that? That is so cool!"

"It was my grandmother's," says Cynthia. "Actually, it still is, but she can't wear it anymore. I'm so lucky that she wasn't as tiny as most of the women from her generation. She was a little bit bigger than average, so it fits me. Neat, huh?" Cynthia is wearing a traditional mandarin-style shantung silk pantsuit. The fabric is shiny red with an intricately stitched pattern of yellow dragons, green pagodas and other ancient Chinese symbols. OK, so it doesn't come straight out of *Vogue*, it is still a really amazing outfit.

"Oh, my God, you've got those adorable little Chinese slippers, too. They are so cool!" I say, listening to my own voice rise a notch. The slippers are also silk, and also covered with embroidery at the tips. And to top off the look, Cynthia has somehow put up her shiny black hair with lacquered chopsticks. It looks really sophisticated. I suddenly feel very clunky and ordinary. A girl with a braid. I wish I had some exotic family heritage to fall back on, but I don't. My great-grandfather was supposedly a Talmudic scholar who ran a big school in Vienna, but as for the women in my family, nobody's been very memorable. . . .

Oh, but who gives a damn about the past? You can't live there, for God's sake.

A song by the Killers is blasting on the CD player in the living room, where people I recognize from Westmore are draped over every piece of furniture, or standing in clumps by the drink table, or huddling around Cynthia's CD collection. The room is so small, with even just fifteen people, it feels densely crowded and deafeningly loud. But that's a good thing, right? I remind myself. C'mon, just behave like a normal teenager. Get with the program. Best years of your life, and all that. I take a deep *zazen* breath.

"Fran!" Leo and Katie surround me and bring me further into the room. I pull a can of Sprite from a big cooler and pop the top. At least it's something to do.

"So that is a very sexy top," says Katie, who's wearing several layers of lacy camisoles over a mini-skirt.

155

"Oh, thanks," I say. Naturally, I'm not going to tell them it's my mother's. But wouldn't she be pleased to know that?

"They make your shoulders look creamy," Katie says.

"And creamy shoulders are a good thing?" I ask.

"Oh, very," Katie says. "Who should you show them off to?" she says, looking around the room. "Let's see—"

"So what's the program tonight?" I interrupt.

"It's going to be stupid, but I guess it'll be fun," says Leo. "Right before midnight, we're all going to put on those stupid pointed New Year's hats and then do the count-down and blow those stupid blowers little kids get at birthday parties."

"Lame, huh?" says Katie. I look around quickly.

"Hey, you don't want Cynthia to hear that, do you?" I say.

"Oh, she agrees with us," says Leo. "Her parents bought all this cheap party stuff in Chinatown in New York—"

"Leo!" I say.

"No, it's true," says Leo. "They have relatives there, and they go back all the time. And there are all these stores that sell weird toys made out of paper and plastic, and stuff."

"I wish we could drink real Champagne tonight," says Katie. "But we have to settle for sparkling cider. Do we at least get to kiss whoever we're standing next to on the stroke of midnight?" She shrugs—then her eyes light up. "Maxie!" Max walks through the throng over to where we're standing and puts his arms around Katie. He doesn't kiss her, though. I think he's too embarrassed. I also think he'd really like to.

"So," I say to Max, "how's the play going?"

"It's cool," he nods, rubbing his thumb along Katie's shoulder. "You gonna come?"

"Yeah, I guess," I say.

"You're not gonna flip out, or run out of the theatre in the middle of any of my big speeches, are you?" I smile uncomfortably. I had hoped he'd forgotten all about that day a few months ago, when I sort of freaked out and walked away from try-outs. I smile and shrug.

156

"No, that was just a mood thing. You know."

"Ugh, girls and their hormones. Really creeps me out sometimes," says Max.

"Oh, Max," says Katie, swatting him across the chest. "You have no idea. We are so superior to the male gender. All those hormones give us super powers, don't you know that?" she laughs up at him.

"Oh, yeah, well super this, Katie-queen," and he swiftly hooks his hands under her arms and swings her around the room, knocking over two open soda cans in the process.

"Uh-oh," says Cynthia, who dashes over. She must have eyes in the back of her head. She mutters something strange under her breath. An ancient Chinese curse, perhaps?

"Oh, sorry," say Katie and Max, mopping at the foaming soda on the rug.

"Look, I'll pay to get your rug cleaned," says Max. He's really not such a complete dolt. "I'm really sorry."

"Don't worry about it," says Cynthia, straightening up. "This rug is really old, anyway—and I don't mean that it's an antique."

Somebody changes the music to something really slow and really old, and somebody else starts turning off lamps. Suddenly the room grows much darker and quieter, as boys and girls pair off. Cynthia's dancing with some guy I don't know—I've never really even seen her hold much of a conversation with any of the guys at school, so I'm kind of surprised. But he's cute; he's not much bigger than she is, but they look good together. Leo is dancing with Jonathan—the tall, skinny, geeky guy who goes around the cafeteria looking for homework hints. Wait a minute, I get it. Brainy Leo helping clueless Jonathan. Oldest story in the book. But what does she see in him, I wonder. She could do much better. Then, just as I'm studying the floor, I feel a hand on my shoulder. I look up, way up, and see Troke, he of the long, usually greasy hair. It's clean and shiny now, thank God.

"Hey, wanna dance?" he asks in a mumbling bass.

157

"Sure," I reply. I wasn't going to stand there in Cynthia's living room and say no. The slow songs are continuing. Stuff I dimly recognize from oldies radio, like Three Dog something and Chicago. I can't remember if that's one group or two. Anyway, here I am, with my arms sort of around Troke's waist—he's too tall for me to put them anywhere else. And he's got his hands around my waist. I can feel the heat of his hands through my sweater. I suck in my stomach. This is weird. Are we supposed to talk, or just dance?

"So, uh, it's a bummer we gotta go back to school Monday, huh," he says. Oh, God, I guess we have to make conversation.

"Yeah, I guess. Whadja do on break?"

"Not much. You know. Vegged. Pigged out. Played touch football with my brothers and cousins."

"Oh, you have a big family?" Listen to me. What a complete dork. I sound like somebody's old-maid aunt.

"Yeah, sorta. We're Catholic."

"Oh." Was that supposed to explain something? Is he stereotyping his own family? I don't really get this guy. I didn't tell him, 'I'm Jewish. My family is small.' So why did he ask *me* to dance, I wonder, as we make slow circles on the living room rug. I didn't think he even knew my name. Maybe he *doesn't* know my name, it occurs to me. Maybe he thinks I'll say yes because I'm the new girl, and must be desperate for attention. Well, at least he isn't trying anything weird. I mean, his hands aren't moving anywhere they're not supposed to. We continue our slow-motion shuffle around the floor. What am I supposed to do now? I look around the room: Cynthia and Leo are still dancing, though they don't look like they're all that into it. Katie and Max are dancing too, and they look really happy. They're whispering and giggling and Max's hands are moving up and down Katie's back.

Then the front door opens again.

"Yo, man," says Max, who's facing the door. I see Carter Brown coming into the room. Sabina is nowhere in sight; clearly, Cynthia did not invite her.

"Hey," says Carter, unwinding a wool scarf and tossing it on a chair. I peer around Troke, discreetly, to get a better look. Carter's light brown hair catches the light; he looks all hunky in blue jeans, and just sort of, well, nice.

Oh, I wish I were not such a pathetic creature—not the rotten piece of fruit I feel like I've become. I wish I were more, innocent, I guess, not corrupted by dirty deeds, by horror, by guilt, regret. . . I just wish I were less complicated.

The song ends and somebody turns up the lights. Immediately, the noise level in the room rises tenfold, as boys and girls uncouple. The coolers are opened and people chug cans of Coke and Sprite and Full Throttle. Brent and some other guy I don't know are muttering about the lack of beer, and begin heading for the door. I watch them slip out wordlessly.

"It's eleven forty-five, everyone," calls Cynthia. Carter Brown has arrived just in time for the grand finale. I wonder if he's been at somebody else's party the whole night. Sabina's? I glance quickly at Troke and go over to Cynthia.

"So, did you see?" she asks me, smiling.

"Of course," I say, hoping no one else catches our drift. I lean in to whisper, "Why did he come so late? I mean, do you think he went somewhere else first?" Cynthia shrugs.

"No idea," she says. "But he said he was coming, and here he is. So get moving."

"Cynthia," I say, "come on. I'm not going to do anything obvious."

"Well, you can go over and say hi. That's allowed."

"But I don't know him. And he doesn't know me." Cynthia begins shoving me, hard, toward Carter Brown. I remember that she's known him forever, so for her, this is no big deal.

"Carter," she nudges him in a familiar way. "Have you met Fran Singer? She's new this year. I'm just introducing her to people she hasn't met yet. It's hard starting over in high school, you know? Or I guess it is, anyway," says Cynthia, breezily.

"Hi," says Carter, sort of looking in my direction. I take this opportunity to notice he's got beautiful blue eyes and an almost square chin—a strong chin, I think.

"Hi," I reply, glancing up into his face for a split second. End of conversation. I have absolutely nothing to say to this guy. I could ask him about *Romeo and Juliet*—I remember seeing him at tryouts, before I fled the auditorium. But that seems lame.

"Well, I'm gonna go get the hats and the blowers, now," says Cynthia, walking away. "Its almost time."

"So, uh, did you just move here?" asks Carter. "I've never lived anywhere else. I think it would be sort of cool to start over someplace new, for a change, instead of the same old boring place." I am so startled that he has addressed a remark to me—why would he bother?—that I'm caught completely off-guard.

"No, I, uh, I've always lived around here, too—down in the city, actually. But I, uh, wanted to come to Westmore, so they let me in." I shrug. That was not stellar.

"Who'd want to come to Westmore on purpose?" Carter laughs. Now he must think I'm a complete idiot. I really don't know what to say—but Cynthia saves me.

"OK, everybody! Take these! Put the hats on!"

"Do we have to?" somebody asks.

"Yes, come on, get in the spirit," says Cynthia. She turns on the TV so we can watch the ball drop in Times Square.

Everyone begins counting: "Ten! Nine! Eight! Seven! Six! Five! Four! Three! Two! One! Happy New Year!" We all blow our little horns—the paper strips unroll like long tongues. Katie and Max kiss. So do several other couples. I'm just standing here a few feet away from Carter Brown, who's now laughing and joking with others. Somebody starts singing *Auld Lang Syne* in a goofy voice, and pretty soon everybody else joins in, trying to remember the words.

Should old acquaintance be forgot,
And never brought to mind...

160

I guess things could be worse. A lot worse.

Good riddance to last year. The new one can't come fast enough.

Chapter 24

Leo's parents' car pulls up to my house at one in the morning. My ears are still ringing from the loud music. My toes are numb from the cold, and from standing in high heels all night. I thank Leo and her dad and quickly make my way into my dark, silent house. I expect everyone's asleep. I find myself wishing my parents had waited up for me, so that I could let them know that I actually had a good time—in my own way. I wouldn't tell them about Carter Brown, of course—they'd only leap to all sorts of bizarre conclusions—but I could tell them the party didn't completely suck. That's all they need to know.

As I put my foot on the first step heading upstairs, I hear a slight noise coming from my right, from the darkened kitchen. My heart starts pounding: Is there a burglar in the house? Is someone there? I stop and walk slowly toward the kitchen, my heart still pounding. I see the black silhouette of a figure sitting, hunching, at the table. It's Mom. I stop a few feet away from her.

"Mom?" I ask softly. "Why are you sitting here in the dark? Were you waiting for me? We said one o'clock, right?"

Mom doesn't answer. I hear her take in a deep breath.

"Mom? Are you OK? What's wrong?" This is the question I have not let myself ask her for months—and now, at last, it slips out. The tired look on her face. The bouts of standing and staring off into space. The frequent car accidents. I don't want to know. Whatever it is, I can't take it on. She's my mother and she's fine, and that's that. I actually turn away and start tiptoeing back toward the stairs. As if, by turning my back, the merest hint of trouble will be banished.

But if anyone knows that's not how life works, it's me.

"Fran," Mom says softly. "Come sit. I need to talk to you."

At one in the morning? This cannot be good.

162

"Do you have cancer?" I ask. "Just tell me. Don't lie, don't try to cover it up. Tell me."

"No, Fran. I'm not sick." She pauses. "I am sick—but sick at heart. I'm not dying."

"What--? Where's Dad? Why aren't you talking to him? Why are you telling me this?"

"Dad knows. We're working on it, together. But right now, he's sleeping. We've been up so late, so many nights, discussing this, and he's worn out from work. It's gotten to me, maybe more than I let him know."

"What's gotten to you? What are you talking about? Mom!"

"Shh! Keep your voice down," she whispers harshly.

I have no idea what's going on here, but my heart is thumping loudly, and I'm breathing too quickly.

"Sit," Mom whispers.

"I don't want to sit. I want to stand." I say this, but I feel my knees begin to wobble. My body already knows something; my brain refuses to.

"I've been getting letters," Mom says. She pauses. I wait. I don't know what's coming, but whatever it is, I don't want to hear it. I want to be a million miles away. I'd sooner humiliate myself by telling Carter Brown I'm hopelessly in love with him, than to stand here right now and listen to my mother.

"I've been getting letters," Mom begins again, "for months. Sometimes several a week." She laughs bitterly. "Thank God you never bother to bring in the mail. I was so worried," she catches her breath, "I was so worried you'd see them, but how could you, they were addressed to me, and you wouldn't know...I don't think you'd recognize the handwriting, anyway—"

It is the babbling that has truly begun to frighten me. Mom is rambling on, not making a tremendous amount of sense. Still, I say nothing, waiting. Peter's training kicks in: I begin taking very slow, deep breaths to calm my racing heart.

163

"In these letters," she continues, "she calls me names. She calls you names. She says horrible, horrible things, things I would never say to a living soul, things I don't ever want you to hear, to read, to know."

I grip the edge of the kitchen table for support. I will myself to remain standing, to take what's coming. It is a missile aimed at me, not my mother.

"I didn't know what to do," she says. I am grateful I cannot read her expression in the dark, cold kitchen. "I've shown your father—some, not all. We've discussed it. We've been at a loss. Until now."

"Now?" I croak, quietly.

"The Vinings are threatening to sue us. I—we, that is, your father and I—we thought we had taken care...that we had done everything to avoid this. But now, they may—"

"What does it mean?" I ask, at a total loss. My mother's words echo, like ricocheting bullets, through my head: *horrible, horrible things.*

"It means, Fran, that this could all come out in the open—in open court, I mean, unless we find a way—"

"You mean," I stammer, "you mean, that everybody has to know? My friends? Everybody?" This is almost too much to bear. No, not almost. It is too much.

"Not necessarily," Mom says softly. "We're not to that point yet."

"Then what? What do I have to do, Mom?" I break out sobbing. I cannot help it. It is as if a wound that had barely begun to heal has been ripped wide open again. "What do I have to do to, to stop the pain? When does it end?"

"Oh, my darling." Mom has risen from the table and taken me in her arms. Dad comes in, his hair tousled from sleep. He see us, he knows.

"Oh, Carla," he says, "was this the best time?"

"I'm sorry, Charlie, I just couldn't, I couldn't—" Mom is crying too, crying hard. Dad grips both of us.

164

"Don't worry," he says. "We'll find a way. We'll find a way to fix everything."

"No!" I say, my voice rising. "You're lying, Dad! I'm not a child! You can't fix this. You can't make it go away. You can't change what I did! You can't—I'm a monster! Just admit it! And I've ruined everything for you, and Mom, and Toby! Just throw me in jail!"

"Nobody's going to jail, Fran," Dad says, in a tone of voice that suggests he knows this for a fact. "And you're not a monster. You're human. You made a mistake. People make mistakes all the time."

"Mistakes! I didn't just make a mistake, Dad! I murdered an innocent child!"

My words hang in the air, like invisible poisoned daggers. I have never said anything like this out loud, to my parents, since it all began. We are silent, stock still. The clock on the kitchen stove ticks, as if nothing has happened. As if time itself can just slip along at its usual pace, without a care.

They say time heals all wounds, but I don't believe it.

The year is new, but I am feeling very, very old.

Chapter 25

They insisted that I go back to school on Monday. As if it mattered. As if I could take any interest in history, or Spanish, or math. If only I could. If only you could solve problems by practicing trigonometry. Cynthia and Leo ask me if I'm all right. I look pale, they say. Is that it? Pale? That's not so bad then. How about broken. Sick inside, sick with worry, and shame.

I lay awake all night on Saturday, the night of our kitchen "conversation," if you want to call it that. My parents had insisted that I try to get some rest. As if. But I didn't want to give them a harder time than they were already having, so I obediently went to my room. At about four in the morning, I got out of bed and sat on my meditation pillow. I thought I would go insane if I did not find a way to turn my mind away from its sickeningly familiar track.

Seated on my brown pillow, I crossed my legs and placed my hands loosely in my lap. At first, I sought only to concentrate on my breathing. To make breathing the only thing in the world that existed, or that mattered.

Just free yourself from all incoming complications and hold your mind against them like a great iron wall.

Peter was right alongside me. I could almost feel the warmth of his bulk, his soothing, reassuring voice.

Quiet your mind.
Reflect
Watch
Nothing binds you.
You are free.

I sat with eyes closed, determined not to get up for a long, long time. Returning to bed was out of the question. I breathed slowly, in, out, in, out. . . . I remembered something Peter told me, about a concept called *dukkha*. It means that life is suffering, life is difficult. This didn't make me feel better—but at least it was relevant. It didn't sugar-coat things. Peter had told me many legends about Buddhists and the Buddha himself. I forgot most of them. But one, I remember, was about *dukkha*. Some guy goes to visit a sage—a wise man who practices Buddhism—and asks him, 'What is the most important truth?' The sage replies that it is *dukkha*. The guy is totally disappointed and asks, 'Is there anyone else up here that I can talk to?'

When Peter told me that little story, I laughed because it rang true. Who *wouldn't* want a different answer? Nobody wants to be told that life is suffering. But it is, isn't it? At least, for me. Peter also said that *dukkha* is all about the ways we complicate our pain through our rush to avoid it—which makes us suffer more. Meditation is supposed to help us—or help me, anyway—to let the pain just be there, inside me like a tumor, where I can look at it— taste, touch, smell, feel it—and then move on past it.

But how?

At school that Monday, after winter break, after beginning a new year that's looking pretty rocky, I feel as if there is a film in front of my eyes. I am so tired. And I cannot think. During House, Christa Neal's voice floats through the air, and I cannot take in a word she is saying.

"So, did you enjoy yourself?" Cynthia asks. She no longer looks as exotic as she did New Year's Eve, now that she's back to jeans and a sweatshirt. For a moment, I have no idea what she's talking about. I blink hard, struggling to return to the present.

"Uh, yeah, it was really fun."

"Did you get to know Carter a little? He's really such a pussycat."

"Uh, not really—but I really appreciate the introduction. He seems nice."

"Well, we'll work something out," Cynthia says, mischievously. "I'll find a way for you to bump into him again. I know!" she exclaims. "There's a dress rehearsal for *Romeo and Juliet* this afternoon after school. Let's go watch, and afterwards, we can go hang out back stage. That way, you'll have something to talk about, with Carter."

This plan means nothing to me. A week ago, I suppose I would secretly have been jumping for joy. But right now, I can't even remember what joy feels like.

"OK, great," I say, trying as hard as anything to sound genuinely enthusiastic.

The rest of the day is pointless. At three-thirty, I head for the auditorium, where I'm supposed to meet Cynthia to watch the play. We find seats in one of the darkened back rows.

"This should be fun," Cynthia whispers in anticipation. I'm wondering how I'm going to keep my eyes open. The rehearsal begins. Bill Kirby, the drama teacher who so fascinated me during the audition last year, whispers last-minute instructions to cast members on stage. Everyone is in costume—Renaissance reds, pantaloons, pointy-toed shoes. Carter doesn't have the lead role. I think he's Mercutio, Romeo's friend. Which means he's on stage early in the play. I fight to stay awake long enough to see him—I owe Cynthia that much, if not myself. But before long, I feel my eyelids closing. . .

I'm in a garden, alone with Peter. It's summer. We're both wearing shorts. The garden is beautiful, filled with bright flowers and shrubs that have been trimmed to look like animals. There are curved stone pathways everywhere, leading into various sections of the garden. I see little stone statutes of a fat Buddha spread throughout the garden. I point to them and laugh. Peter smiles and nods. Then, as I watch his face, he turns serious.

"Push away the disturbing thoughts," he says.

"What?" I ask, watching as one of the little stone Buddhas gets up and begins dancing. I'm not frightened by it. Instead, I'm amused.

"Push away the disturbing thoughts," Peter repeats. "Healing comes from the mind." And then I hear a loud noise. I wake with a start. There's a busy sword fight taking place on stage. The actors are grunting and exclaiming as they thrust their plastic swords at one another. I look over at Cynthia, who's watching the play with an amused expression.

Suddenly, as clear as day, I know what I must do.

Chapter 26

I wait until the house is completely quiet, and I think that everyone—even my parents—is asleep. Not a word about Saturday night has been spoken in the last three days. They haven't said anymore, and I haven't asked. And Toby, of course, knows nothing. My pure, innocent brother. He'll never understand that I really do love him.

I dress as warmly as I can, and pull an extra blanket out of the linen closet to bring with me. My rubber-soled hiking boots—chosen for their sturdy warmth—are noiseless as I slip downstairs and out the front door. I have not been down the block in a long, long time. In the pitch black night, with only a handful of street lights for guidance, the familiar houses look eerie and threatening. I forgot to bring a flashlight. Oh, well. I cannot turn back now.

Oddly enough, the powerful exhaustion that has practically paralyzed me has suddenly lifted. I have huge amounts of adrenalin coursing through me. For the first time in a long time, I know exactly what I have to do, and why.

I reach the Vinings' house. It almost looks darker than the others. My breath is coming in short bursts, but I must keep going. This much I know for sure: the house stands empty. They have gone away; I don't know where. I suppose I'll never see them again. I walk slowly toward the front of the house, then veer around to the right, where a stone path leads to the backyard. The pool, which I have not seen since that day last summer, is covered over. The cover sags in the middle, where autumn leaves have collected.

I approach the gate that surrounds the pool. My whole body begins to tremble now, and I am overcome with an urge to vomit, but I take in large gulps of cold air, and the nausea subsides a little.

"*Chod.*" I say this word out loud. I do not know how to pronounce it, exactly, so I guess. It doesn't matter. *Chod.* It's an ancient Tibetan word. Peter has taught me this. It means "cutting through." Cutting through fears to bring freedom and peace of mind. Peter told me, you visualize the most terrifying demons, ghosts, and ghouls, to create an atmosphere of pure horror. You invite them in. In ancient times, he said, people did this in cemeteries, and forced themselves to picture all sorts of horrible things involving skeletons and blood. They were terrified. And that was the point, Peter said. They forced themselves to face their worst and deepest fears, because the only way to master them, or put them behind them, was to confront them head on.

So I spread the blanket I brought on the hard cement next to the pool gate, and pull up the edges to wrap around my legs. And I wait. This is the place. The source of unimaginable horror. And I have decided I must confront it, or I will never be free of it. I do not expect to forget what has happened here, ever, but if I let it keep me—to wrap me in its cold, death-like embrace—I will never be able to lead a normal life.

The night is cold and still. I can feel the tip of my nose slowly freezing. But I will not leave. I am waiting. If I cannot win the battle here, I can never win it anywhere.

I force myself to look out at the pool, and to relive every single moment of that afternoon, right up to the moment when I had finished cleaning the house and had come out to see if Theo was still asleep in the hammock. He was not, of course. Tears stream down my cheeks. They would freeze, were it not for their salty warmth. I just cry, and cry, and cry.

I can never bring Theo back. I can never go back and undo that day, or the moment when he must have wandered over to the gate, and, entranced by the sparkling water, climbed up and over. I always knew he was a climber. I should have known. Should have. Would have. Could have.

But I did not. And I have to find a way to move on.

171

I continue staring out at the blackened pool. A cold breeze stirs the dry, brittle leaves gathered in the middle.

This is what I remember next: a hand gently shaking my shoulder. My mother and father, their faces inches away from mine, looking at me with love and concern. And then another pair of feet, large feet in torn sneakers, on my other side. Peter. Slowly, I lift my stiff, sore body up off the concrete. My nose is clotted with snot. My bones ache. And I begin to shiver. It must be morning, but I don't remember sleeping. Weak sunlight shows the true outlines of the swimming pool in mid-winter. Abandoned. Useless. Harmless.

My father removes his coat and wraps it around me. Gently, wordlessly, they help me to my feet. I stammer out a question.

"How did you know where to find me?"

"Dad got up to check on you in the middle of the night," Mom says. "He said he had a feeling. I don't know. When he saw that you hadn't even gotten into bed—"

"I was terrified," Dad says. "I couldn't imagine—I looked all over the house for you."

"And then we stopped to think. Where on earth would you go? I looked to see what was missing—your coat, your hiking boots. So we knew you'd be outside somewhere."

"We left Toby and just started wandering around the neighborhood—"

"And then it hit me," Mom said. "It seemed like a long shot, but I thought you might actually have come down here. I wasn't sure, but—"

"And then your dad called me," said Peter, who was now standing beside me. "And I thought for a moment, and told him about *chod*, and what that might mean to you."

"And now, we want you to come home," adds Dad, gently.

I don't know what to do. I don't know now the right thing to do.

"Do you think it worked?" I ask Peter.

"What do you think?" he replies.

"I'm not sure. How do I know?"

"Fran," he says. "Do you remember *sukha*?"

I frown, struggling to remember.

"It is the opposite of *dukkha*," Peter says, gently. "It is joy."
He recites:

"When suffering overwhelms me
I will breathe in
And leave an opening in this moment
For the joy that lies just behind it. "

I take a deep breath, and my chest hurts. Peter has triggered another memory, something Helen Keller once said: "Although the world is full of suffering, it is also full of the overcoming of it."

I can never bring Theo back. But I can try to learn to live with it. And I can begin again. That much I can do. And for now, that is more than enough.

THE END.

CPSIA information can be obtained
at www.ICGtesting.com
Printed in the USA
LVHW020001230721
693426LV00012B/894

9 781087 902036